Archie cleared his throat and turned to the wall. He pointed at two bricks, longer and narrower than the rest. "Around this same time, another legend started about these bricks, referred to as the Roman Bricks. They are a shade of pink, not red like the rest, and it takes two stacked one on the other to make them the same height as the others."

A lighter-colored mortar filled the space around them, as though to patch a hole. If Archie had not pointed them out, Sam wouldn't have noticed them.

"Roman Bricks? Hmm." She shuffled to get closer. Dad had mentioned bricks.

"Bricks?" Nicole crossed her arms. "Pft."

Sam nudged Nicole. "Pay attention, or Mrs. Phelps—"

Nicole shook her head, but her frown remained.

Sam had to get closer to those bricks, but a stack of wood and an old door with Koko Hair Tonic painted across the top leaned against the wall. Yellow "caution" tape cordoned off the area around the wall. How could she examine them with all that junk in the way?

"So, what's that legend about?" a gray-haired man asked.

Had he read her mind? She tensed, waiting for the answer.

"I thought you'd never ask." Archie rubbed his hands together. "Legend has it that they came from Romania when the Romans dominated Europe. Experts say the mica dust in them gives them their glow, but it's rumored that magic is stamped right into the clay."

The Disappearing Names

by

Avis M. Adams

The Disappearing Names

Cover Art by *Jennifer Greeff*

The Wild Rose Press, Inc.
PO Box 708
Adams Basin, NY 14410-0708
Visit us at www.thewildrosepress.com

Publishing History
First Edition, 2023
Trade Paperback ISBN 978-1-5092-4590-1
Digital ISBN 978-1-5092-4685-4

Published in the United States of America

Dedication

For Sine and Amahle. I will love you through all time.

Acknowledgments

In any writing endeavor, there are a host of writers behind the scenes critiquing, cheering, and listening to the mad ravings of the author. It is to these folks I tip my hat. To the Baker Street Group (Ardi, Harvey, Skeeter, and Gary), I couldn't have gotten through the first drafts without your astute observations and suggestions! The Flamingos (Carl, Wendy, Catherine, and Melanie), you kept my POV issues at a minimum! And finally to my friends at TWRP, especially Ally Robertson, and the Debut22 email group, thanks for all the support, the beta reads, and the line edits! Dang that pesky grammar stuff!

Chapter 1

The OPU Tour

Monday. Sam's least favorite day of the week, and this one made her head pound. If she could only quit replaying her parents' fight over and over—

He'd been gone a week, ever since Mom found that key, and Mom had been in a trance ever since. It was like she never woke up and Sam had become invisible to her. She shuddered. She needed to get Dad back. That was all she wanted, her life back, and yet here she was on her way to the Old Pioneer's Underground Tour.

The bus joggled over the bricks in Pioneer Square, while Dad's voice mingled with Mom's in her brain. Mom shouting about the key, and the lavender scent on his clothes, and Dad mumbling about disappearing names, bricks, and the family Bible. Was he talking about Aunt Eli's Bible?

"OPU, OPU," Nicole chanted.

Derrick picked up the chant, and the bus erupted in chaos. Sam grinned. Nicole's antics kept Sam sane. The summer program had three field trip choices, Pike Place Market, Seattle Center or OPU, and each class got to choose. Sam could not have cared less, but Nicole wanted the underground tour. Dad had said no. He didn't want her going underground, but he didn't have a reason, or he wouldn't say what it was. So, that decided it. Of course, she had to go.

Why didn't he want her to go, though? At least she wasn't headed to the stuffy classroom. The bus hit a pothole, and she bumped her head against the window. Perfect, a lump on her forehead, that was all she needed.

Disappearing names, he must be talking about the ones in Aunt Eli's tattered, old Bible. It was falling apart, and the print faded, right? But Mom was crying, and Dad said names were disappearing—not fading. He'd cracked open her door, as if she hadn't heard them fighting. His eyes were red as he sat on the edge of her bed. "Go to the Space Needle or Pike Place Market, just not underground."

He frowned, and she glared, then he rushed out, dropping a little black key tied to a purple leather cord. She bent down and lifted it from the floor, the scent of lavender filling the room. She opened her mouth to tell him, but he was gone.

A girl at the back of the bus screamed, and Mrs. Phelps jumped from her seat behind the bus driver and marched down the aisle. Sam gazed out the school bus window at a deep blue sky. Sam leaned her head against the window. Lavender. Maybe a couple of rain clouds would appear and cheer her up. She pressed her fingers to her temple. If only she'd interrupted them, screamed, done something, anything, maybe Dad would have stayed.

Mrs. Phelps moved back down the aisle, checking homework. Sam slumped back in the seat waiting her turn. She pulled the key from her pocket. It was short and stubby with a funny tab at the end of a hollow tube, but what was it for? A fresh burst of lavender tickled her nose as she held the key by the leather cord. It was part of whatever was going on between Mom and Dad. Could it bring him back?

"Homework?" Mrs. Phelps held out her hand.

Sam pulled a sheet from her bag. How did she end up in summer school anyway? Ah, yes, Baxter of the dreamy gray eyes and dark hair curling over his forehead. She'd wasted a whole semester laughing at his horrible jokes and helping him with his homework and not turning in her own. Heat rose to her cheeks. They hadn't even kissed, and now he was on his way to Texas A&M, and she was stuck on this bus. Mrs. Phelps marked her paper and handed it back, moving to the next row.

She sighed and slipped the paper back into her bag. Happy birthday, Sam. Wasn't sixteen supposed to be special? How could it be with Mom in a trance and Dad gone? She'd missed his chocolate chip birthday waffles.

The key, disappearing names, lavender, they all meant something, but what? She sighed, her thumb caressing the key. If she had enough time to figure this out, would Dad come back? She gazed at the brick buildings as the bus passed by. There was never enough time.

The brakes squealed as the bus jerked to a stop in front of the Pergola. Mrs. Phelps stood and waited outside counting heads as students piled off the bus. Sam shook her head. She had to focus, or she'd fail summer school too.

"The Pergola is one of Seattle's most famous structures. It used to be a streetcar stop in the early 1900s." Ivan grinned.

She rolled her eyes at Ivan and shuffled after Nicole.

"This way people. Stick together." Mrs. Phelps led

them to a door and stood guard as students shuffled through. Why did they have to listen to another lecture? Mrs. Phelps had done enough of that. Couldn't they just start the tour already? It would be dark underground. She could blend with the shadows and work on her plan to get Dad back. What if she could just go back in time and hide the key before mom ever found it? Then there wouldn't be a fight, and Dad would never leave.

How would she do that? Time travel? Right. She ran her fingers over the key stuffed deep in her pocket as sun dappled through the trees in Pioneer Park. A clock chimed 10:00, and the clank and rustle of shop owners opening shutters and doors began. Laughter tinkled through the air as tourists in front of the totem pole took "selfies," and the aroma of hamburgers and fries floated on the breeze, but she had no appetite. Dad's last words still confused her.

"The names are disappearing," he'd said. "All the Greats."

The disappearing part made no sense, but "the Greats" were her ancestors, the great grandparents, family who had come from the old country, but how were the names disappearing, and what did it mean? Somehow it was all connected. Sam stared into space.

"Sam, this way." Mrs. Phelps frowned.

Sam shook her head. Mrs. Phelps's field trip notes were fifty percent of the grade for today. She had to focus.

She filed into Doc Maynard's Public House and settled on a bench next to Nicole, whose frizzy hair swarmed around her head like a nest. Nicole pushed up her glasses and grinned at her. A woman in an "I Heart Seattle" t-shirt, coffee stains covering the heart, crushed into the seat next to Sam. The bench creaked, and Sam scooted closer to Nicole.

Sam gazed into the darkness of the ceiling where the carved wood of the antique bar disappeared. She counted twenty-six people reflected in the bar mirror, and fifteen of them were her classmates. A young man with striking amber eyes and red hair sauntered into the room.

"Welcome to the Old Pioneers' Underground Tour, ladies and gentlemen." He wore a black t-shirt with Underground printed in white letters on the front and Old Pioneers on the back. He had on old fashioned plaid slacks that bagged at the knees. They exposed his gray socks and scuffed brown leather loafers.

Sam pulled out a tablet and pen and crossed her legs. At least he was on time.

"I'm Archibald, and I'll be your guide today. You can call me Archie." He paused. "Before we begin, I'd like to set the scene with some history of Old Seattle."

Sam's eyes grew heavy as Archie's speech droned like a hive of bees. "After Seattle's Great Fire in 1889, the city fathers wanted to rebuild Seattle—raised the sidewalks to the second story of the buildings—first floors still exist below the sidewalks—those rooms are what we are going to explore today."

When would he get to the ghost stories? She jotted down a few names and dates that Mrs. Phelps would want to see in her notes. She always said, "You will learn more history through the stories of the Underground, and doing the research will help you retain them."

Phelps-y was right. Sam got sucked into those ghost stories of murderers, disappearances, and robberies.

Nicole nudged her, and Sam dropped her pen.

"What?" Sam glanced at her then at the clock on the

wall. It had been fifteen minutes already?

"Watch him. This guy is weird." Nicole frowned at Archie.

"Weird?" Sam stretched her neck to see over Ivan. Archie's amber eyes didn't blink or make eye contact with anyone. Then he glanced at her, and the hair on her arms stood on end. Was he staring at her? He tucked his red hair behind his ears and pointed to the old photographs on a back wall. Where was Mrs. Phelps?

"Did he just wink at you?" Nicole clung to Sam's arm.

****

Archie strolled to a door and swung it open. "This way ladies and gentlemen." He led the group to the top of a wooden staircase.

She crossed her arms, plodding along with the group. Nicole put her arm through Sam's. "You only cross your arms when you're angry. What's up?"

"Nothing's up." Sam dropped her arms and gave Nicole a fake smile. Should she tell Nicole about the key, her parents' fight, or her plan? Sam didn't even have a plan yet.

Archie counted heads. "Twenty-six. We are all here, so let's head underground, ladies and gentlemen. Watch your steps."

Nicole clutched Sam's hoodie as they descended a dark staircase that led to a dimly lit hall. Light filtered through the purple stones in the sidewalk above them, giving Nicole's face a pale cast. They were below street level, and age-old dust filled her nostrils like the dry wood and dust of Grandma Stewart's cellar. Grossie.

Archie stood at the far end of a wide hallway. One bare bulb hung from the ceiling. She ducked around a steel girder that reinforced the timber beams to support the building above them. Ivan and James took turns leaping to slap the beams overhead, releasing dust and spider webs.

"Eww. It's in my hair." Nicole bent over and brushed her fingers through her hair.

Sam brushed at her hair. Spiders didn't bother her, but those two better watch it. Mrs. Phelps called Ivan, but it was too late. A fine powder filled the air, and Sam sneezed and flicked grit from her shoulders.

Archie leaned against a door frame, a layer of dust covering the wooden walls and the light bulbs. Sam tripped over a patch of uneven cement in the packed earth as the group pressed around Archie, raising a cloud.

"This is the Pioneer building which held the Seattle branch of the Portland Trust and Savings, and the vaults were right here." He pointed to a corner, and Sam stood on tiptoes to get a better view.

"The year 1901, as many of you know, was the time of the Alaskan Gold Rush, and many gold mining companies had offices and vaults here too." Archie glanced over people's heads. "How many of you have heard the story of 'The Bank Robbery that Never Happened' or 'The Murder with No Bodies'?"

"I've heard of them." Ivan raised his hand. James slugged him in the arm, and some of the tourists laughed.

"What a suck-up." Sam rolled her eyes.

"Two very famous legends, for sure." Archie stuck his hand in his pockets. "They went something like this:

"In 1901, Big Jim and Red McClusky, two Portland residents, charged into the Trust and Savings in Seattle, their guns drawn." Archie mimicked drawing pistols from holsters. He pointed his fingers, like gun barrels at the crowd, and the crowd took a step back. A woman stepped on Sam's toe.

"Ow—"

Mrs. Phelps shot her a frown and tilted her head. Sam bit her lip.

"They must have known that Mr. Charles Stickel Esq., manager of the Seattle and Portland offices, was in town that day. A guard tried to stop the gunmen, but he failed, and Big Jim and Red broke into Mr. Stickel's office. Shots were heard." Archie motioned with his fingers as if shooting. "When the dust settled, the guard searched for Mr. Stickel, but he was gone. Poof. But so were Big Jim and Red." He blew the tips of his fingers.

"That was over the top." Nicole raised an eyebrow at Sam.

Sam rubbed the key in her pocket. She'd read this story, but still it gave her goose bumps. Where did they go?

Archie cleared his throat. "Yet, all of the gold was still in the open safe. The Bank offered a reward, and William Meredith, Police Chief at that time, organized a search, but neither Mr. Stickel nor the robbers were ever found."

Mrs. Phelps pulled Ivan and James to the far side of the room.

"I wasn't whispering." Ivan tugged, but Mrs. Phelps held tight hissing in his ear.

Archie waited for silence. "All three were presumed dead, but a week later, witnesses reported seeing Big Jim and Red in this very building." Archie paused then lowered his voice. "Or maybe it was their ghosts."

Silence hung in the underground space, and Nicole slipped her hand into Sam's. Archie scanned the room, his gaze landing on Sam. Footsteps echoed in the dark hall behind her.

"What was that?" Nicole clung to her.

Sam peered down the hallway. "It's a trick, Nicole." She swallowed and turned toward Archie, whose gaze remained focused on Sam's face.

"What the—?" Sam stared into Archie's amber eyes.

Archie cleared his throat and turned to the wall. He pointed at two bricks, longer and narrower than the rest. "Around this same time, another legend started about these bricks, referred to as the Roman Bricks. They are a shade of pink, not red like the rest, and it takes two stacked one on the other to make them the same height as the others."

A lighter-colored mortar filled the space around them, as though to patch a hole. If Archie had not pointed them out, Sam wouldn't have noticed them.

"Roman Bricks? Hmm." She shuffled to get closer. Dad had mentioned bricks.

"Bricks?" Nicole crossed her arms. "Pft."

Sam nudged Nicole. "Pay attention, or Mrs. Phelps—"

Nicole shook her head, but her frown remained.

Sam had to get closer to those bricks, but a stack of wood and an old door with Koko Hair Tonic painted across the top leaned against the wall. Yellow "caution" tape cordoned off the area around the wall. How could she examine them with all that junk in the way?

"So, what's that legend about?" a gray-haired man asked.

Had he read her mind? She tensed, waiting for the answer.

"I thought you'd never ask." Archie rubbed his hands together. "Legend has it that they came from Romania when the Romans dominated Europe. Experts say the mica dust in them gives them their glow, but it's rumored that magic is stamped right into the clay."

A tingle ran from the back of Sam's head down her spine. Some of her Greats came from Romania, right?

Laughter filtered through the dim underground. Archie ignored the scoffs. "Each year on the anniversary of the robbery, the Roman Bricks come alive, and ladies and gentlemen, that happens to be this very day, July 7th."

"My birthday?" She clamped a hand over her mouth and glanced at Mrs. Phelps who kept her attention on Ivan and James.

What had Dad said about bricks? Oh, yeah, the Greats had brought bricks from the old country along with the Bible. Did the bricks have something to do with the names disappearing? She put her hand to her head. That was too crazy to be true.

"How do they work?" Chuck would get points for that question.

She bit her lip and leaned forward to catch every word.

"No one knows for sure. People have disappeared since the time of Mr. Stickel, though, and there are rumors that time travel is the reason." Archie's eyes narrowed and his smile disappeared.

Her heart began to race. Time travel? This was what she needed for her plan to work.

"Time travel, my butt." Nicole snorted, breaking Sam's spell.

Others were murmuring in the closeness of the

hallway. They didn't believe the story. Maybe they didn't want to. Did Archie sense that she wanted to believe? She met his steady, green-eyed gaze.

"A girl about your age," Archie pointed at Nicole, "disappeared in 1961."

Nicole took a step back.

Archie pointed to a framed newspaper article. A photo captured the image of a girl with a heart-shaped face and a dimple in her chin, her dark hair short and curly.

"A reporter traced the 'Roman' Bricks to a pioneer family in Portland. It turned out the bricks were relics from the old country, but how could they make people disappear? The reporter never found out. Perhaps the family had a secret to keep."

A secret? About time travel? Sam had to know the secret of the Roman Bricks. Maybe she could use them to go back and hide the key from Mom before she ever found it? A whiff of lavender escaped from her pocket as she gripped the key.

"The fronts are smooth from being touched," Nicole whispered.

So, others had tried. The caution tape enticed rather than deterred people from touching them. Was this a ploy by the OPU to attract people to their tours? Maybe, but Sam itched to test her theory.

Nicole clasped Sam's arm, shaking her head. "I know that look. Don't even think about it."

Sam pulled away from Nicole, her gaze on the bricks.

Ivan raised his hand. "Why wasn't this on the news?"

"It was in 1961. That was before the Old Pioneers

Underground even began." Archie yawned until his teeth showed. "My advice? Don't touch those bricks." Archie jabbed a finger at Ivan who jumped. Archie grinned.

Every hair on the back of Sam's neck stood on end. This guy was up to no good.

Archie brushed dust off his shoulder. "You can find more about the robbery, murders, and the Roman Bricks in our book, *Stories of The Old Pioneer's Underground,* which is sold in the gift shop at the end of our tour." He glanced at the bricks then turned and walked away, the group shuffling after him.

"This way, watch your step." He helped a woman through the doorway, his lips moving as though counting heads. He stopped at Sam. Was Archie singling her out?

She glanced at the bricks. They seemed to be glowing. Had they been glowing this whole time? She had to test them. If they didn't work, she'd have to think of something else. What did she have to lose? She ducked behind a huge beam. Nicole followed, her mouth open and ready to speak. Sam held a finger to her lips, and Nicole froze. The last of the tour group disappeared through the door.

"Don't do it, Sam." Nicole took her hand.

Mrs. Phelps charged through the door, Archie scurrying on her heels. "I'm telling you they are not with the group." She scanned the walls and beams of the area.

Did Mrs. Phelps notice the glow? Sam's body went rigid, and blood pounded in her ears.

"But I counted everyone. I'm sure they're with the group." Archie leaned around the beam where Sam and Nicole huddled. He winked. "Besides they are your students. They wouldn't dare misbehave, right? Now, come on. I'm on a strict schedule." He took Mrs. Phelps by the elbow, and he led her through the door.

"What's Archie up to?" Sam turned to Nicole, but Nicole's eyes were clamped shut.

"I saw nothing. I heard nothing." Nicole tugged away. "If we hurry, we can catch up to the group and tell Mrs. Phelps we were there all along."

"I have to try. It's like they are calling to me, and that scent—If I could just go back to the day—"

Nicole grabbed Sam's arm. "That was just a story."

Sam pushed Nicole and reached for the glowing bricks. Nicole tripped, pushing her, and as her hand landed on the Roman Bricks, the air whooshed from her lungs.

Chapter 2

The Lucky Star

Sam pressed the heal of her hand against her temple, but the room still spun. She sat on a dirt floor, standing was not an option, yet. She rubbed her eyes and scanned the room, wooden shelves lined one wall, the mellow smell of new wood filled the air.

Where was that stack of dusty old wood, the door with Koko Hair Tonic written across the top? Where were the Roman bricks?

"What happened?" Nicole sat on the floor holding her head in her hands.

"Nicole?" Sam squinted into the dim light. *What happened to that lightbulb?*

"I don't feel so good." Nicole rubbed her tummy.

"We must have fallen." Sam cleared her throat to mask the quaver in her voice. She pushed herself off the floor.

"Why is it so dark?" Nicole rocked on the floor holding her midriff. "Where is the caution tape?"

Slender beams slanted through the cracks in the ceiling. They were still underground. Footsteps crossed the floor above. Footsteps? That wasn't right. Sam spun around. Wooden stairs led up to a door, but they weren't the ones she'd used to get down here.

She strained to find something familiar in her

surroundings, not the wooden ladder leaning against one wall, or the three wooden barrels in a row by the shelves, or the five kegs stacked near the stairs. A small mud-splattered window let in filtered light from the top of a brick wall. Rows of wooden crates stood stacked under the window. The floor was swept, and there wasn't a speck of dust anywhere.

"Why did you have to touch those bricks?" Nicole moaned as she got to her feet. She pulled her cell phone out of her pocket illuminating stenciled letters on the crates.

"Lucky Star Saloon?" Sam hadn't read anything about a Lucky Star Saloon.

Nicole snorted. "Lucky my butt. Dang. No bars. Crappy service." The green tinge from the light of her phone lit Nicole's frowning face.

Sam shrugged her shoulders. "We're still underground, so the group can't be far." Maybe if she acted like this was normal, Nicole wouldn't freak out. The sooner they rejoined Mrs. Phelps' class the better, but she needed someone to reassure her. Where were the bricks? This wasn't anything like the room in the tour, and why was Portland stenciled under Lucky Star Saloon on all the crates? She shook her head. *Get a grip.* "The group is down here somewhere. We just have to find them."

Nicole wrinkled her nose. "I smell fish."

"You and your nose." Nicole could sniff out chocolate from 500 paces. "Can you smell us back to the group?"

"How do I not have bars?" Nicole held her cell phone up. "This is starting to fr—"

"I know. It's amazing, right? Must be part of the

tour. I felt the air being sucked right out of my lungs." Sam avoided Nicole's eyes.

"No, it is not amazing."

She needed a plan. One that got them back to the group, back to the room with Koko's Hair Tonic. Somewhere not here.

"This is that stupid Baxter's fault. If it wasn't for him, we wouldn't even be in summer school." Nicole frowned.

"Now wait a min—" Sam grew warmer by the second, and she clenched her fists. Why did she have to bring up Baxter now?

"We're lost because of you. Again. Mrs. Phelps, our class, and Archie are long gone." Nicole jabbed her finger at Sam.

"And who might you be?"

Sam spun around. Blinded by a flickering light, she reached for Nicole's hand and gripped it. Nicole dropped her phone into her pocket.

"It's just a kid," Nicole whispered pulling her hand from Sam's.

"Are you with OPU? Can you help us?" Sam stepped back as the light came closer.

"Oh, pee, you? I do not—" The boy shrugged. Why was he holding a lantern?

"You know, Old Pion—"

"Cut the crap, kid, and turn on the lights." Nicole's eyes darted around the room.

Oh no. Nicole was melting down. Sam had to say something quick.

"Look, Nicole." She pointed at the bricks glowing on the wall. "I'll just touch them again, and they'll take us back to the group." She reached out her hand.

"Group? What group?" The kid stepped closer, holding the lantern.

"Where's Archie?" Nicole backed into a row of barrels.

"Archie?" The kid shook his head.

"You know, our tour guide?" Nicole blinked her eyes and squinted.

Sam glanced over her shoulder. Was someone whispering? No one was there, but the bricks glowed. Sam was drawn to them as a familiar scent surrounded her. Lavender. She longed to touch them.

The boy cleared his throat, and Nicole scoffed. He was in an old-fashioned costume with short pants and a flat cap.

"This is a joke, right?" Sam's hair rose on the back of her neck.

Nicole held out her hands. "Fess-up, kid. You came here with a lantern in these old clothes to scare us. Now take us back. Please?"

"Costume?" The kid clutched a giant ring, several brass keys clanked as he shifted from foot to foot.

Nicole's frown grew deeper. "Portland is stenciled on all these boxes. Why not Seattle? Where are we?"

Sam backed away from the boy, but the room was crowded with crates and boxes.

"Seattle?" The boy's head tilted.

"Where is that pile of boards? Where is the tour group? Where—" Nicole clutched Sam's sleeve with shaking hands.

"Nicole, it'll be okay." Sam loosened Nicole's fingers from her sleeve. She turned in a circle, scanning the brick wall, the new wood beams, the barrels, and boxes stacked in rows. "We just lost the group that's all.

This kid can help us find them, right, kid?"

"There had better not be a group in this stockroom, or you boys will be in big trouble."

Sam glanced at Nicole and back at the boy. "Excuse me? We're not—"

He shook his head and held the lantern higher. "If Mr. Lawrence learns you have broken into his stock—"

"Wait. What?" Sam put her hand to her head to stop the spinning.

"First, no bars, then Portland, and now Mr. Lawrence?" Nicole put her face in her hands.

"Nicole. This is not Portland." Sam took her friend's hands in hers. Nicole's eyes were huge, and tears glistened, threatening to fall.

Sam held Nicole's gaze, but Nicole's chin began to wobble. If they both started crying, who would get them out of this mess? "We just need to keep clam." Sam braced herself. Would her word game distract Nicole?

"Clam? If you mean calm, say calm, but I just want to go home." Nicole glared at Sam, tears rolling down her cheeks. "Now."

"I'm not sure what you're talking about." The kid held up the lantern, hiding his face, "Tell me how you got in here, and I might not tell Mr. Lawrence."

Sam took Nicole's trembling hand in hers. How could they be in Portland, and who was this Mr. Lawrence? The bricks glowed brighter on the wall, and Sam took a step closer. Maybe if she touched them, they'd take them back to room with Koko's Hair Tonic on it?

She tightened her grip on Nicole's hand and reached up to the glowing bricks. "Please take us home," she whispered and pressed her palm against the bricks.

****

The bricks glowed with less intensity, as footsteps sounded above the Lucky Star storage room. Sam glanced at the yellow wood of the shelves and the stairs that should be gray and dusty. They filled the room with a clean scent of fir. Nothing was the same as room on the tour. She hit her hand on the bricks, but nothing happened. Why was nothing happening?

She glanced over her shoulder at the boy. He stood holding his light, frowning.

"No, no, no." She beat the bricks with her fist. This had to work, but the glow of the bricks had disappeared. Maybe if she pressed harder, the group would appear, and everyone would laugh at them. Sam would laugh along, anything to get back to electricity and cell service.

Nicole clung to Sam's sleeve. "Hurry, Sam. Mrs. Phelps has to know we're gone by now." She sniffled. "I want to finish this tour and go home."

Sam turned to look at the boy carrying the lantern. She had to do something fast, or she'd join Nicole and lose it. "The bricks aren't working, so this kid has to show us back to the tour, right kid?"

"Bricks? Tour? What are you talking about?" The boy's voice was clear and confident.

Sam pushed her shaking hands into her pocket. She gripped the key and rocked on her heels.

"So, Mr. Lawrence is your boss?"

"He is."

"I see." Sam paced the floor in a small line back and forth. "And what is your job?"

"I run his errands." The kid lowered the lantern, his cheeks smooth as satin in the golden light.

He's young. Sam nodded. She could outsmart this

kid. "Mr. Lawrence must be rich."

"Mr. Lawrence is half-owner of the Lucky Star Saloon."

Sam's plan was running out of steam. If this kid was acting, he deserved an Oscar. Sam had to catch him in a lie. Then he'd have to take them back to Archie and the tour. She glanced at his shorts. "Mr. Lawrence can't afford long pants?"

"I procure my own attire from the laundry." He shuffled his feet.

"Laundry?" What did she say now? Nicole gripped her arm like a vice, and she was at a loss. "Can't your parents afford clothes?"

The kid stared at his shoes. Sam had hit a nerve, and she tensed. Why didn't he say something, anything? No. That wasn't true. She wanted him to tell her this was all a gag, a joke, a big trick they played to make the tour more exciting.

"My parents are none of your business."

"What?" This kid was hiding something. Sam had to try a different approach. "Don't you have to be twenty-one to work in a saloon?"

His back stiffened. "I had my sixteenth birthday in April." He glared at Sam his hands his on hips. "Now quit changing the subject. How did you get down here? Nobody can get in from the tunnels without this key." His voice cracked as he jangled a key ring on his belt.

He was Sam's age, but his voice hadn't changed?

"I-do-not-believe-this. Where is Archie?" Nicole stomped her foot and frowned at Sam.

Sam rubbed her face with her hands, a tingle of gooseflesh shivered down her back. "Where are we?"

"We are in the Lucky St—"

"I know that." Sam clenched her fists. If she heard Lucky Star Saloon one more time, she'd scream. "But where is that?"

"On Yamhill and 3rd."

"Yamhill?" Nicole grasped Sam's arm. "Sam, there's no Yamhill in Seattle that I know of."

"Seattle? This is Portland." The kid's face was a mask of shadows. His lantern swayed as he spoke. "Oregon."

"Portland, Oregon?" Sam staggered. His answers didn't add up. Was he part of the tour or not? Sam lifted her hand to her chest her blood pounding through her veins.

"This can't be Portland" Nicole glared at the kid. "That's three hours south of Seattle."

"Three hours?" he scoffed. "It takes three days on a fast horse at the very least." He lifted his lantern and frowned.

"This can't be happening." Sam's fists shook at her sides. This had to be a joke, right? And if Ivan and James were behind this, they were in big trouble.

The kid planted a hand on his hip and glared at her. "If you won't tell me how you got in here," he headed to the stairs, "I must tell Mr. Lawrence."

He couldn't leave them here. He was the only way out.

"Maybe we should talk to Mr. Lawrence." Sam held out both hands and the kid hesitated. It was time to play along with this trick and meet Mr. Lawrence. Anything to end this, this—whatever this was.

Nicole grabbed Sam's arm. "This would never have happened if you had listened to me." She glared at Sam. "I tried to stop you."

Nicole was right. She had touched those bricks and now they were here. The kid moved toward the stairs. She whispered to Nicole, "Play along."

"Could you show us a way out of the tunnels?"

He stared at Sam, his face blank. Would he help her or not? Sam couldn't take much more of this. She rubbed the muscles in her shoulder and whispered to Nicole, "Once we are on the street, we can make a run for the school van and wait for Mrs. Phelps."

Nicole nodded. Sam stared back at him.

"I will listen, but first explain how you got through the padlock on this door."

Sam scanned the storage room. A hinged door in the ceiling gave her an idea. It had a rope tied to the handle and disappeared through a hole in the floor.

Sam pointed at the ceiling. "We must have fallen through that hole in the floor and passed out."

"Why didn't you just tell me the truth?" The boy scowled. "I'll show you the way through the tunnels." He turned.

Nicole and Sam followed him through a door set in a brick archway, which he locked behind him. He led them through another arch, and they turned right down a hallway then left and then right again. Sam was lost. Nothing looked familiar. "Are you sure this is the way?"

"I use these tunnels to meet Paul and Will after work, so yes, I am certain this is the way."

Cobwebs hung from the beams, but the smell of freshly cut wood filled her nostrils. Sam lost track of all the archways and doors and different tunnels that connected them, but a trail of footsteps led into the darkness of the tunnels. Were they from the tour group? If not, who had made them?

He lifted the lantern to light the way. "I'll take you out by the river."

"The river? Don't you mean Puget Sound?" Nicole's brow creased.

"Puget Sound?" The kid stopped, the lantern swaying in his hand.

His frown made the hair on Sam's neck raise, but there was something else, his soft voice, his smooth face, that niggled in Sam's brain. He was older than he appeared, but he didn't move like a boy.

"Right, the river, that's perfect." Sam nodded at Nicole.

Nicole stomped her foot. "The river is not perfect." Her voice rose. "We don't want the Willamette. We want Puget Sound." Nicole shook her head.

Sam stopped. "What is today's date?"

"It's Sunday."

Sam shivered. It was Monday. Nicole's mouth hung open, but she didn't move. Was she in shock? Sam was.

The kid turned with the lantern illuminating his face from below his chin. His eye sockets had that dark, dangerous look that Dad got when he held the flashlight under his chin to scare her.

"Sunday?" Sam's voice trembled and she put a hand to her throat. What was happening?

"Sunday, the 6th of July. Why do you ask?"

"But the tour was on the 7th." Sam took a step but stumbled. She grabbed the wall beam for support. Her stomach did a flip. Had the bricks worked? Had they sent her back in time? One day wasn't enough, though. She needed a week if she was going to destroy the lavender-scented note.

Nicole took a step toward the boy. "What year?"

Nicole squeezed her eyes shut

Sam wet her lips.

"It's 1901. Why do you ask these questions?" He stared at Nicole as if she had two heads.

Sam's knees wobbled and she clutched Nicole's arm tighter. Had they gone back over a hundred years?

"Stop kidding around." Nicole shook her fist at the kid.

"What is *kidding around*?" he asked.

The walls pressed in on Sam, and she held her chest. She took Nicole's hand and whispered. "Archie said the murder happened in 1901, right?"

"Right." Nicole clutched her hand. "That's the year Mr. Stickel disappeared with the robbers."

Sam grabbed her shoulders. "Mr. Stickel—"

The kid swung the lantern around. "Mr. Stickel?" His hand shook and the lantern flame flickered. "The other owner of the Lucky Star?"

"He owns the Lucky Star?" The words were out before she could stop them, but a new plan began to formulate.

The kid held the lantern higher. "How do you know him?" Without warning, he turned and walked briskly down the tunnel. "This is a farce. Quit wasting my time. I must return before Mr. Lawrence notices I am gone."

Nicole gasped. "Sam, if we lose this guy, we'll never find our way. We could wander in these tunnels for years."

Sam ran after the kid who didn't slow down, dragging Nicole behind. "Mr. Stickel sent us down here from Seattle."

He stopped. "Why?"

Sam blinked. "He's worried about his money."

"Yeah, his money. You know how he feels about his money." Nicole's voice wavered.

"Everybody knows that." The kid frowned. He looked from Sam to Nicole waiting for further explanation.

"You better take us back to the stockroom." Sam stared at the kid. This had to work.

A frown formed on his smooth face, and he rocked from foot to foot making the lantern flame flicker in the darkness. "First you want out of the tunnels, now you want back in the stock room?"

"I know. It's confusing, but now that we know about your connection with Mr. Stickel, you can help us help him." Sam waited, crossing her fingers behind her back.

He dipped back. Sam reached out to steady him, but the kid didn't fall. He spun and ran into the dark passage, taking his lantern with him.

"Quick." Sam grabbed Nicole's hand. "If we lose him, we're really lost."

Chapter 3

Girls Will Be Girls
1901

Sam pumped her legs as hard as she could, slipping on the uneven floor as she went. This was nothing like Seattle. Was this Portland like the kid said? Was Nicole right? Were they three hours south of Seattle? But they had gotten here in a flash, and the bricks had been glowing. So, had she traveled through time? Nicole was right, a fishy odor did fill the air. It must come from the river. Sam stumbled over a piece of wood lying in the tunnel and gasped. She couldn't lose him.

"Stop, please." Her heart pounded like a bass drum as she ran. "We promise not to tell Mr. Stickel we got into the stockroom." She reached out and caught a handful of his shirt. They tumbled onto the dirt floor. The lantern flew from his hand, hit the ground and the flame went out. Sam's eyes adjusted as light filtered through cracks in the floor above them creating inky shadows.

"Unhand me, you scoundrel." He slapped Sam's hands and scooted away.

Darkness honed Sam's senses. "Ouch." She jerked back. If she were him, she'd run away too into the dark. What could she say to him that didn't make her sound like a crazy person?

He climbed to his feet. "I must return to the Lucky

Star before Mr. Lawr…" He glanced over his shoulder. Sam saw tears glistening as he moved his head from side to side. Why would he cry? She glared at him. If he planned to run again, she was ready.

"You're still playing this Mr. Lawrence game?" Nicole's sharp voice startled Sam. "Just stop it, already. If we don't get back to the tour before it's over, we're in bigger trouble than you, so quit messing around."

Did Nicole still think this was a prank? Sam rubbed her skinned elbow.

"My clothes are filthy." The kid brushed at his pants, smearing mud. "Hairy Larry will insist on sending me home to clean up, which means he will dock my pay."

"Hairy Larry?" Nicole glanced from the kid to Sam her brows scrunched into a frown.

"I did not mean to refer to him in that derogatory manner. He despises being called by that name, even if it is highly accurate." He picked up his lantern and reached into his pocket. He struck a wooden match on the wall and soon light filled the space once again, and Sam could make out his facial features. Was he trying to make sense of Sam and Nicole, just as they were trying to make sense of him? Could one-hundred-plus years make understanding one another that difficult?

Sam stared at him. He spoke funny, his clothes were odd in an old-timey way, and these tunnels had a whole different smell. Maybe the bricks had worked. Her pulse pounded and dizziness made her knees wobbly. 1901? She'd wanted to go back two weeks. Why had they gone back so far?

The kid broke her reverie.

"Mr. Lawrence checks the accounting books on Sunday. I must be there with the keys." He turned. "He hates to be kept waiting.

"You're leaving us?" She needed a different approach, something that would shock him into revealing he was working for OPU. There was something about this kid that didn't add up.

"You're Mr. Lawrence's assistant, right?" Sam waited. What was it about him?

"I am his errand boy, not his assistant," he said, his voice rising.

Sam peered at him. The light flickered from the lantern casting a glow on his face, and Sam grinned "You're not a boy."

His mouth dropped open, and his jaw worked but no words came out. "I...I..."

"You're a girl." She'd hit a nerve, and the boy, or girl, shifted from foot to foot. "Help us, please. We need to get home."

"I am not a girl." The kid's voice cracked, and the lantern swayed as he moved back a step.

This was a girl, and that explained the tears. Sam took a step toward her. "What's your name, and why are you pretending to be a boy?"

The kid wiped his eyes and pushed his chest out. "I am not a—"

Sam shook her head. "You're crying, and your voice is soft. Unless you're butch." What was he hiding?

"Butch? What?" Tears rolled down his cheeks. "Okay. My name is Henri, not Butch."

"No. I mean—" Sam shrugged. "Never mind. We just want to know why the disguise?"

Henri glanced at her feet, and her shoulders slumped. "You are correct. I am a girl, and I must wear this boy's attire, obviously, because girls can't be errand boys."

Nicole stared at Henri as though she had two heads. "Girls can do anything a boy can do."

"That is not true." Henri wiped at her tears and shook her head. "I am afraid if Mr. Lawrence found out I was a girl, I would no longer be employed."

"So, if you're a girl, why do they call you Henri? What's your real name?" Nicole stood with her hands on her hips.

"Henrietta, but Papa has always called me Henri. That's what gave me the idea to dress as a boy." Her tears fell in earnest now. "I need to find my papa."

A jolt of pain ran through Sam's chest. Just mentioning her papa made Henri cry even harder. "This is about your papa, isn't it?"

Henri nodded. Her sniffles filled the silence. Sam waited until she could speak.

"He's gone."

Sam reached out a hand, but let it drop. "How long has he been gone" She waited for Henri to go on. Sam's own father's face loomed before her, his sad eyes as he said goodbye tightening her stomach. Henri's step faltered as she spoke.

"Five days ago. He left for the bank, the Portland Trust and Savings, but he never came home. I haven't seen him since."

"The Portland Trust and Savings?" Nicole grabbed Sam's arm. "That's the bank Archie said got robbed."

Henri's face was in the shadows, but Sam could see her shoulders rise as her muscles tensed. Nicole's words upset her, but why?

"I became a boy to help my father." Henri wiped her nose on her sleeve. "I went to the police, but they thought

I was hysterical. They laughed at me, and one leered at me. I ran home and made the decision to look for him myself."

Sam shook her head. "They wouldn't help at all?"

"No, so I went to Misa at Yabuki Laundry. She hears about the comings and goings of people as they drop off their clothes. I thought she might know something about Papa."

Nicole stood with her arms crossed, but she didn't argue or interrupt, so that was a good sign. Sam nodded for Henri to continue.

"Misa helped me get these clothes, and she cut my hair, so I'd look like a boy. That way I could look for Papa down by the docks. It's safer to be a boy." Henri shuddered.

"That gives me an idea." Sam glanced at Nicole, who was shaking her head.

"No, no, no. No ideas, no plans, no touching anything, Sam. You'll just get us into more trouble." Nicole pressed her lips together, her arms crossed over her chest.

Sam squinted at Nicole. Why couldn't she just listen for once? "You haven't heard my plan yet." She turned to Henri. "Maybe Misa has boys' clothes that me and Nicole can borrow, then we can help Mr. Stickel, too."

Henri tapped her chin with her finger. "Misa might be able to help you with the clothes, but Mr. Lawrence would have to hire you, and I—"

Nicole grabbed Sam's arm. "No. We have to stay close to those bricks and quit talking about Mr. Stickel."

Sam glared at Nicole as she pulled her arm out of her grasp. Sam turned to Henri, but Henri had a frown on her face. Sam's throat went dry. Why did Nicole have to argue over everything?

"Your names." Henri stood with her hands on her hips.

"What?" Sam scratched her head. Where did their names come from? Hopefully not her family Bible.

"I do not know your names," Henri said. "If I'm going to help you help Mr. Stickel, I need to know who you are."

Sam sighed. Nicole hadn't ruined everything after all.

Sam held out her hand. "I'm Sam." Henri just stared at her. Sam swung her arm to Nicole. "And this is my best— my partner, Nicole."

Nicole frowned at Sam, her eye twitching. Well, maybe not best friends or partners after today. Their shuffling in the tunnel had raised a dust cloud. Had time stopped? She waited for Henri to respond.

"Sam? That is a boy's name." Henri didn't move a muscle as she stood holding the lantern, one hand on her hip.

"It's short for Samantha, a nickname."

"So, you and Nicole need to dress like boys because you are helping Mr. Stickel, but that doesn't add up." Henri put a hand on her hip. "Here's what I think. You don't even know who Mr. Stickel is. Tell me the truth."

How did she know? Sam wobbled, as blood rushed from her brain. Now what? That was plan G already. "Okay. Okay." She paused. "I think Mr. Stickel has something to do with the bricks in the Lucky Star stockroom. Archie called them Roman Bricks, and I believe we need them to return home."

"Bricks? So, you don't know Mr. Stickel."

"No."

"But if I help you, you will use the bricks to go home?"

"Yes. We just want to go home. Can you help us?" Should she have mentioned the bricks? Done was done. The tension in her neck and shoulders eased as the truth poured out of her, but would it help them get out of this mess? This had to work. They were out of options.

"The Roman Bricks." Henri's stony glare unsettled Sam. "Misa mentioned them to me once, but they are dangerous."

"Misa knows about the bricks?" Sam didn't expect Henri to have any information about the bricks, but if she could just meet Misa—

"Can you tell me what Misa told you? Anything we learn about the bricks will help us get home."

"I'll tell you what I know. The first day I worked in the Lucky Star Saloon, I saw Mr. Frederick Meyer III set them in the wall. He wasn't a mason, so I thought it odd and mentioned it to Misa. She told me that the Meyer family owns some magic bricks that are really old and valuable."

"How does Misa know all of this?" Sam tapped her chin with her index finger. If this information was true, it was worth more than gold.

Henri smiled, and Sam took a step back. Her smile transformed her. She was beautiful, and no boys' clothes could hide that. It could be her downfall.

"I will bring you to Misa. This is the tunnel that leads to the washroom of the Yabuki Laundry."

"So, you'll really help us?" Sam tensed. *Please don't say anything, Nicole. Please.*

"Yes," Henri said.

"Wait. I don't want to meet Misa. I want to go to the

stockroom and the bricks." Nicole took a step toward Henri a look of determination on her face.

Sam stepped between Nicole and Henri. "Just listen." Sam clenched her teeth. Nicole twirled her hair around her finger, which was never a good sign.

"No. I'm done listening to you. I want to go home, not to the Yabu-bah Laundry."

"Don't worry, Nicole. This is the only way to get more information about the bricks, and they are the key to getting us home." Sam kept her voice low, trying to calm Nicole. Nicole stopped pacing and Sam turned to Henri.

"Okay, Henri." Sam needed to talk to Misa, and soon, or Nicole was going to ruin their chances of getting home for good.

****

Sam stuck close to Henri, who held her lantern leading them through a dark corridor and into another room. Moving through the tunnels behind Henri was like following Archie through the OPU. At least she was helping and not trying to get away. Maybe Sam could help her in return? They both wanted their fathers back, and she felt bound to Henri. Nicole would have to understand that, but blind trust didn't come easy for her. At some point, she'd have to work with them, not against them. How would she make that happen?

Nicole plodded along behind Sam. "Why do you have to work?"

"It's one way to look for my dad. It keeps me close to the waterfront, plus it gives me money to buy food and lodging since Papa left."

Henri stared into the distance, her shoulders slumping. "I'm afraid he was taken by a crimper."

"Crimper?" Sam stopped.

"What's a crimper?" Nicole cocked her head waiting for a response. She seemed more interested than worried.

"Crimpers are people who drug unsuspecting men and put them on ships who need crews. They earn up to fifty dollars a man." Henri's voice cracked and her eyes shone with tears.

"You mean shanghai." Nicole seemed oblivious to Henri, as her frown grew deeper. Maybe this would help keep her mind off time travel and magic bricks.

"Shank-eye?" Henri wiped her eyes.

"No, shanghai. It's when a person is drugged and put to work on a ship against their will, like you said a crimper did."

Henri's tears began to fall. Was Nicole thick as a brick? Her words rocked Sam, too. Hadn't she shanghaied Nicole? She always got Nicole into trouble. Was she cursed or just curious? All she knew, was she had to help Henri find her dad, get Nicole home, and get her own dad back. She sighed. Dad. He's what got her into this mess.

Nicole put a hand on Henri's shoulder.

"Shanghai sounds precisely like a crimper. By the time the men wake, they are out to sea and cannot swim to shore. The men must work on the ship for months or even years. Hardly any of them see their homes or families again. That is why I sought employment with the Lucky Star. Its access to the tunnels and waterfront might enable me to find my father before he's put on a ship. There might still be time."

"Time?" Sam asked.

"If a crimper captured him, he could still be in the

Portland tunnels somewhere. They do not always load the men on a ship right away."

"Oh, my goodness." Sam shuddered and put a hand to her chest. The dull gleam in Henri's eyes made Sam shiver. Did she have the courage to help Henri against crimpers? "We might be able to help."

"You can?" Henri wiped her face with a bandana.

Sam nodded. "Start at the beginning."

"Well...father didn't come home after work five days ago."

"Did you check at the bank?" Nicole would ask the obvious, but they had to start somewhere. Sam bit her lip and waited.

"Actually, I left out some important information. Papa didn't work at the bank. He was following a lead because, you see, he works for the United States Secret Service." Henri hung her head.

It had taken a lot for Henri to trust them. She was desperate. Sam pulled Henri into a hug. Henri pushed away and wiped her eyes. "If I do not tell you this story quickly, it might be too late. Whatever happened to Papa involves Mr. Stickel somehow." Henri wrung her hands. "When I made inquiries at the saloon, Mr. Lawrence offered me a job, which I found odd, but when I found out Mr. Stickel is part owner, I knew I was getting close. I have friends, Paul and Will, who are helping too. They practically live in the tunnels and have shown me how to get from the Park Blocks to the waterfront and how to avoid the dangerous areas."

"Dangerous areas?" Sam's mouth went dry. She put a hand to her throat. Why did there have to be danger? Her throat seemed to close.

"Of course, there's danger." Nicole frowned at Sam.

"I heard rumors about some Roman Bricks and people disappearing. What if my dad was one of those people? That might be better than meeting with crimpers." Tears gleamed in Henri's eyes.

"Hmmm, I think you're right. Mr. Stickel is somehow connected to the bricks. Maybe finding out more about the bricks will help us find your dad and get us back home." Everything pointed to those bricks. Sam shuddered.

"Misa said Frederick III was seen, by whom I do not know, and neither does she, but he was seen setting the bricks with Mr. Stickel. My father disappeared that very day, and Mr. Stickel hasn't been seen since."

Sam put her hand around Henri's shoulder. "So, you believe the bricks sent your father and Mr. Stickel somewhere. Have you tried to use them?"

"I can't find them." Henri stared at the walls as though the bricks might appear.

Sam's fingers began to tingle. She'd used the bricks and got Nicole in this time travel mess. Now she had to help Henri find the bricks and use them to find Henri's papa, Mr. Stickel, and get her and Nicole home. Nicole joined them in the huddle.

Sam cleared her throat. "Let's get those boys' clothes."

Nicole gasped. "Wait, remember Archie's story about Mr. Stickel getting murdered by Big Jim and Red McClusky?"

Sam shrugged and shook her head waiting for Nicole to continue. Henri froze, her face white as chalk. Sam tensed. Now what?

"Red McClusky? That's my papa." Henri fell to the floor the lantern rolling from her fingers. The glass shattered and the flame went out.

The dim beam of light crossed Henri's body where it lay. Why hadn't she paid more attention in her first aid class? What did she do, mouth-to-mouth?

"Is she alive?" Nicole's voice fell in muffled tones.

Sam held her face in her hands. Had Nicole finally accepted Henri and the tunnels? Nicole took Henri's pulse. Sam sank to her knees beside Henri. How did they get her to regain consciousness?

"She has a pulse, and I think she's breathing, but we can't move her." Nicole sat and cradled Henri's head in her lap. "I've got water." She pulled off her backpack.

"Good. Water is good." Sam nodded as Nicole pulled out her water and dabbed Henri's face.

"You two will bring Hairy Larry down here with all that racket," Henri mumbled and pushed herself from the floor.

Sam jumped to her feet. In the dim light, Sam could see tear tracks on Henri's dirt-smudged cheeks.

"You said something about my father?" Henri kept her voice low and cautious.

Sam glanced at Nicole, then back to Henri. Would she pass out again? Sam had no choice. She had to tell Henri what she knew no matter what happened. "We heard about Red McClusky from Archie in Seattle, but we didn't know he was your father." Sam ran her finger along her lower lip, her stomach churning. What forces were at work here, and how was this connected to the bricks? "Was your father after Mr. Stickel?"

"He was. He was meeting his partner, Big Jim." Henri sniffed. "They disappeared together."

"Archie mentioned both those names in the story he told us. We didn't actually see them." Sam didn't want

Henri to faint again, so she let that news sink in before she continued.

"What happened in this story? Is my papa in Seattle then?" Henri asked.

"He might be." Sam glanced at Henri. Would she faint again? "You said today was July 6, 1901?"

"It is." Henri held her hands as if in prayer.

"Well, Big Jim and Red McClusky showed up in Seattle on July 7th, 1901, which is tomorrow." Sam held out her hand to stop Nicole's interruption.

"Showed up? What do you mean, showed up?" Henri, eyes large, leaned toward Sam. "Is this some kind of magic?"

"I don't know if it's magic, but I think it involves the bricks. The important thing is whatever happened to your dad hasn't happened yet, so maybe we can stop it." Sam took Henri's hand in hers. "Take us to the stockroom where you found us, please, Henri. That's where the bricks are, and they may help us find your father and get us home."

"If they will help me find my father, then let us hurry." She jogged into the dark tunnel.

Sam held Nicole back. "If the bricks are glowing, we will be home in time for supper."

Chapter 4

The Murders

Sam jogged after Henri. What did she expect to find in the Lucky Star stockroom? The bricks, of course, but how did they work? Henri raced down a long straight stretch of tunnel, then a sharp right turn, A loud rumble brought Henri to a stop.

"What's that?" Sam put a hand to her throat. The noise was constant.

A burly man with huge forearms and a grizzled beard glared from his forge through the door where Sam stood. A shiver ran through Sam as the man turned back to his table and turned a stone wheel, grinding a piece of metal.

Henri held a finger to her lips and glanced into a room lit by a lantern. "That's the smithy. You don't want to disturb him. Now, be quiet and come on."

"What—" Nicole peered into the room.

"Shh!" Henri grabbed Nicole's sleeve and pulled her past the door.

They raced down the tunnel, past a ladder leaning against a wall, and turned right. Henri stopped in front of a door with a brass lock.

"I didn't think we'd gone that far." Sam huffed and puffed, her hands on her knees.

"We have arrived at the storage room." Henri pulled

the key ring from a pocket and unlocked the door. She pushed the door open, and Sam stepped inside, scanning the walls. Lucky Star Saloon was stenciled on wooden boxes and kegs of rum.

Henri twisted her hat in her hands. "If you can help find my father, I'd be—" Henri mumbled, choking back tears.

"Don't thank us yet," Sam said, placing a hand on Henri's shoulder. She held back her own tears. "It sucks to lose a Dad."

"Sucks?" Henri sniffled. "I do not understand your meaning."

"I mean it hurts." Sam wiped her eyes. She scoured the walls looking for the Roman Bricks. What stood out to her, though, was the trapdoor that she'd told Henri they'd fallen through. Now its presence loomed ominously above her.

She pointed up. "Why is that there?"

"The trapdoor in the Lucky Star?" Henri frowned. "Everyone knows about the door in the floor. Most saloons have one, but still, men fall victim to its treachery."

Nicole scratched her head. "But why do they need a trapdoor?"

Nicole stood beside Sam. Sunlight outlined the shape of the door in the floor of the saloon. Sam could make out a spring, and a rope attached to a latch ran into a hole. Was it positioned behind the bar? Sam shuddered. What a devious way to take advantage of unsuspecting people.

"Does Hairy Larry hold the other end of that rope?" Nicole asked.

"He hates being called Hairy Larry, so never call

him such to his face." Henri frowned at Nicole. "And, yes, he does have the other end of that rope because he is the bartender and a crimper."

"I don't think I ever want to meet *him*." Nicole backed away from the trap door.

"So, Mr. Lawrence is half-owner of the Lucky Star, the bartender, and a crimper?" Sam walked to a spot under the trapdoor. The rope was frayed from being pulled through the hole. "He's a busy fellow, isn't he?"

"In the past week, I have seen Mr. Lawrence mix a powder in the drinks of five men. When the man passes out, Mr. Lawrence pulls the rope, and the man falls through the trap door. From the storage room, the men are loaded into a hand cart and taken unconscious to a place I have not been able to find. If I could, I might find my father."

"Wow." Sam shook her head. The image of men falling through that trap door made her cringe, but she was here to find the bricks. She scanned the walls. Where were they when she needed them? If she ran her fingers over the brick wall, would they appear? Nicole joined her. Henri watched as if in a trance.

"Look. There it is." Sam's voice echoed off the timbers.

Nicole looked up to where Sam pointed. "Where?" Nicole scanned the wall. "I couldn't see them in Seattle, either."

"There," Sam said, pointing to the bricks that glowed. Sam watched their eyes scan back and forth never stopping on the bricks. Sam reached up to them, but they were too high on the wall. "If I could just—"

"Do you want Mr. Lawrence to hear you?" Henri glared.

Sam clamped her hand over her mouth. "Sorry. Didn't mean to say that so loud." How was she going to reach those bricks? She searched the wall. "We could stack some of these boxes." Sam grabbed a crate. It clanked but she couldn't lift it

"I have a ladder." Henri reached behind the stairs.

Nicole grabbed it and leaned it against the wall.

Sam climbed but stopped and gazed down at her friend. This had to work.

"This is it, Nicole." Sam kept her eyes on the bricks. "They're glowing."

"Wait for me," Nicole climbed up behind Sam.

Henri cleared her throat, and Sam gazed at her. "If we see your father, we'll tell him we saw you."

"Thank you." Henri waved. "I wish you success."

Sam climbed higher. The ladder creaked and slid. Nicole fell to the floor, and the ladder rocked. Sam grabbed for the wall, her hand hitting the bricks. A familiar whoosh shook her whole body as the air rushed from her lungs, and Nicole's "No, no, no," echoed in her ears.

****

Sam landed hard on the ground, jarring her teeth. She leapt to her feet coughing and peered through the dim light. The dust, the steel girders, the stack of wood, she was in the room where it had all started. She brushed her hands off, her senses heightened.

"Nicole?" she whispered, trying to slow her heartbeat.

Silence.

She spun in the dark. "No. No. No."

"Nicole." Where was she? She'd done it again. Put Nicole in danger. Sam sank down onto the pile of lumber. At least Nicole wasn't alone in 1901, but could Sam go back, and could she trust Henri? And what was Sam supposed to do now that she was back in Seattle?

"There you are, young lady. You are not supposed to be here."

Sam sank against the wall, but someone had seen her. Who? Sam couldn't place the voice. She slipped behind the woodpile.

"I saw you hiding there."

A shiver ran down Sam's spine. It was Archie, the tour guide. His flashlight beam cut through the dust. The shortness in his voice raised her blood pressure. He was angry.

She curled up as tight as she could to fit behind a Jerry's Cherry Soda sign leaning against the wall, but Archie shone the light right on her.

Every muscle in her body tensed ready to run, and her throat was too tight to speak.

"I only want to help you." Archie grabbed for her.

Grabbing wasn't helpful. Sam jumped up, tripping over the stacked wood. What would he do if he got hold of her? She gained her balance. A yellow wall with the word SEAMSTRESSES in tall green letters drew her attention. She ran for it, with Archie breathing down her neck.

"Wait. Don't go. I've been searching everywhere for you and your friend. You didn't touch those bricks, did you?"

"Bricks?" Sam pressed against the wall. So, Archie knew about the bricks? What else did he know? That she'd gone back to 1901 and that Nicole was still there? He seemed desperate to catch her, but Sam couldn't let that happen. She had to get back to Nicole.

"Stop." Archie glared at her, his amber eyes never blinking, and licked his lips. "Where is your little friend?"

She backed away, keeping Archie in her sight.

Archie stood with his hands on his hips. Had he lost her? She'd been in bad situations, but this was the worst. She gripped the key, its warmth a comfort. She had to concentrate or she was doomed.

"I told you not to touch those bricks, but I knew you would." His face angled toward her, his eyes mere slits in his face.

How did he know, and why did he never blink? Sam kept Archie in sight as she inched through an opening in the wall.

"The story of the bricks is more complicated than what I tell the tour groups, though."

Was Archie lying? Did he know she'd gone back to 1901 and returned? How would she help Nicole if she got caught?

"I'm so glad I found you." Archie rubbed his hands together.

He scanned the sign and wall as though searching for her. He had not found her. She could still get away. Her heart hammered in her chest.

"Just tell me where your friend is. Then you can go home."

Home? Sam frowned at Archie, her mind racing. That's right, she was in the present. She could just go home. But without Nicole? Never. She couldn't just leave her in 1901.

Mom and Dad must know she was missing by now. She was going to be on restrictions for the rest of her life. What did she have to lose? "So, what if we touched those bricks?"

Archie's head snapped to the sound of her voice. He took a step toward her. "We need to talk, Sam." Archie took several more steps toward her. He reached for her again, but she jumped up and sprinted down a hall.

A red door on her left stood ajar. She plowed through it and pulled it closed behind her. She was in a room with a light shining at the far end. She ran to it. Archie grunted, rattling the red door. She dodged into a side passage and crouched under a stairwell. The door had stuck. How did she get so lucky?

"Big Jim, I need your help." He was still stuck behind the red door.

Sam pulled her legs to her chest. "Big Jim?" Did Archie know him? Were they working together?

He gave up on the door, and his voice got quieter as he mumbled. She groped her way deeper into the passage; an occasional bare bulb lighting the way. Had Henri lied about her dad? How was Archie connected to them?

"Archie?" a man called, but his voice came from somewhere closer.

A sudden coldness hit her like an iceberg. Her breath caught in her throat, and she struggled to eavesdrop. Who was speaking? She clutched her chest. Was she having a heart attack?

"Don't hurt her you little weasel," the man said.

She held her hand over her mouth to stop from crying out. Dad? What was he doing here? Was he working with Archie? Sam sank into the dark corner. Had he used the bricks?

"She can't go far in that direction," Archie said.

They shuffled down the passage as light beams lit

the walls and filtered through the cracks missing her by inches. Her nose tickled, and she pinched it tight, waiting for the men to pass by. One sneeze would blow her cover.

"Did you find him?" A third man said.

"We have a complication." Dad was in charge? "There are also two girls down here."

"You knew what might happen if you used the bricks to follow him." Archie grunted. "We all want to get back to Portland, right?"

"I do. Nothing here makes sense to me." The third man's voice was a low growl.

Who was "him?" And could that be Henri's dad? Sam pressed her hand on her chest. If nothing here made sense to him, he must be from 1901 because that's exactly how 1901 was for her.

"We've lost her." Archie was involved, but how? The men mumbled words she couldn't make out.

She sank back with a sigh. Now what did she do? She'd found Henri's dad, but what was Dad doing here? Why would Archie be helping, and if Archie knew Big Jim and Red McClusky, was he part of the murder without any bodies and the bank that was never robbed? Sam clutched the key. Wait.

If they used the bricks, no wonder the bodies were never found. The murder had never really happened, and the bank was never robbed. She sat as still as she could, her sneeze long forgotten as the voice grew louder.

"Archie is not much help." Red's clipped words seemed to thud off the walls.

"He's worried. It makes him cranky." Dad sighed.

"I heard that." Archie had moved down the hall. "Keep your eyes open. We need to find those girls before we can proceed with the plan."

They were leaving. Sam shrank under a stairwell. They hadn't found her, but she couldn't relax, not yet. Archie was involved, but why? Sam shivered, her brain swirling. Her stomach tightened. Why were she and Nicole a complication?

The purple skylights in the sidewalk let in light, and the silhouettes of Archie, Big Jim, and Red disappeared down the passage. If she could only figure out which way led to the street, she could make it to the school van. Home was so close. She crouched down, her head in her hands. Dad was here in disguise, and Henri and Nicole were in 1901. She had to find those bricks and get back to 1901. Henri needed to know about her dad.

Footsteps echoed down the hall. Oh no. Were they coming back? The hair on the back of her neck stood on end, and she hugged her knees into her chest. Could she get back to the bricks? Only if she was invisible.

Chapter 5

Yabuki Laundry

"No, no, no, no, no. Sam?" Nicole slapped the bricks, jarring the ladder. It lurched, and she stopped pounding against the bricks and leaned against the wall.

"Where did she go?" Henri whispered, her voice hoarse.

Nicole shook her head, staring at the bricks. "I have no idea, but she's left me behind. Again."

Henri started to back away. "I better return to the Lucky Star. Mr. Lawrence—"

"No." Nicole jumped off the ladder. "Don't you leave me, too."

Henri glanced from Nicole back to the bricks. "I will stay, but where is Samantha?"

"That's the million-dollar question, isn't it?" Nicole stared at Henri for a moment. "I don't understand the bricks, but together maybe we can figure them out. We have to—"

"Misa did mention the Roman Bricks when I asked her about my father." Henri glared at the bricks. "I had no idea she was speaking about something real. I thought she was telling stories."

Did Henri know more than she let on? How could she make Henri tell the truth? Henri's hand shook as she held the lantern. If she made Henri uncomfortable, she might dash into one of the tunnels and disappear. Nicole shuddered. She wanted to go home, so she'd better stick with the original plan.

"So, what about those boy-clothes?"

Henri stared, her mouth slack. Was she in shock? Yes, but she closed her mouth and led Nicole through a room, turned right, jogged down a long corridor, then she turned left. Nicole kept track of each turn. Maybe she could remember some of the route this time? The moisture in the air turned the dirt floor to mud under their feet.

"It's so humid here." She slipped but caught her balance.

"Yabuki Laundry's boiler pots are down here. They put out a lot of steam." Henri didn't stop. "They are famous for getting white shirts whiter."

"Yabuki is a weird name for a laundry." Nicole hurried to keep up with Henri.

"The owners are Japanese. It is their surname." Henri frowned over her shoulder. "The Yabuki family are good people, and I don't care what others say about them."

"Wait. What do others say?" Nicole stammered.

"I will not repeat what they say. Just know that Misa Yabuki is my friend, and she will find you clothes. Then we will find a way to get to Sam. I am formulating an idea." Henri kept a quick pace yet wasn't breathing hard.

Nicole put a hand to her chest. Her heart was pounding. She couldn't afford to lose Henri and pushed herself to a jog. Between Misa and Henri, she'd learn what she needed to learn about those bricks and find Sam.

"Misa will be in the back hanging laundry. The

steam is thick and will hide our presence. We will be safe."

"Safe? Is there danger?"

"Besides the crimpers?" Henri swung the lantern as she rounded a corner. "They won't catch us."

"Huh." Were the walls getting closer? She stopped, and Henri waited for her. Could she trust Misa Yabuki, and why was Henri running? Nicole nodded to Henri, and they continued their march into the damp darkness. Why hadn't she worked harder in gym class?

Was it her imagination or was the mugginess increasing? Sweat ran down her back, and her palms became clammy. Henri said it would, but sweat ran into her eyes as she raced after Henri.

"Are we there yet?" Nicole asked.

Henri didn't seem to get the joke. Henri jogged down the tunnel as though immune to the heat and humidity. Were those voices? The muffled sounds became louder, then quieter again until she couldn't hear them anymore. Must be workers in other business stockrooms and storage rooms getting supplies and cleaning up. What else could it be?

"There it is. See that light?" Henri pointed into the darkness.

"No." Nicole wiped her eyes. She stopped and put her hands on her knees as she wheezed. "Can we rest for a minute? I can't breathe, and I'm getting an ache in my side." Had they been running for thirty miles? How far did the tunnels go?

"Oh-my-aching-eyes," Henri said. "And all you do is complain. Do you realize how much trouble I am in because of you?"

"I know." Nicole gasped. "I'm sorry."

"I accept your apology," Henri said. "The laundry makes it hot and humid, but we have to keep moving. It is not much farther, I promise. You can rest when we get to Misa and the laundry. Then I must return—"

"Wait. You must return where?" Nicole frowned at Henri. "We have to stick together. I can't take much more of this eternal dark, the humidity disorients me, and now you want to leave me with a stranger?"

Henri held up the lantern and stared at Nicole. Was that another waver? Was she getting ready to run again? She couldn't lose Henri now. The tunnels were alive with voices and figures working and lurking, and Nicole didn't want to find out what they were doing the hard way.

"Your safety with Misa is assured."

"But—"

"I must return to the Lucky Star."

Exhaustion washed over her like a wave. Sam was the one who loved chaos and adventure. Nicole didn't. She missed her friend, but was it better that she was gone? No. What was she thinking? Sam was the one who could get them back to Seattle.

"And Mr. Lawrence must not know that you are here. I will return shortly."

"Okay." Had Henri said he mustn't know she was here? Why mustn't he know? She was just a fifteen-year-old girl from the future. No threat to anyone. Tears threatened to fall, but she cleared her throat. What was Henri's plan? Did Sam really go to the future, and would she come back? Would Nicole be stuck in 1901 forever? She wiped her nose.

"Here," Henri said and held out a hanky then turned and began jogging again. "The heat down here makes my nose run too."

Nicole blew her nose as she raced after Henri, who didn't even look back.

"This is a fine mess, you've gotten us into, Sam," Nicole muttered.

The bricks had brought them to 1901 and Portland, but why had they taken Sam away again? And where did she go? Seattle, or some other city? She could be in San Francisco, London, Rome, or some other city.

****

Sam ducked into another room. Boxes were stacked four high and she found a space to hunker down behind them. She curled into a tight ball and the running footsteps kept running right past her. They slowed. Her legs began to shake. She wanted to run, but she knew her best plan was to stay put so Archie wouldn't find her. She couldn't get too far from the bricks, or she'd never get back to 1901 and Nicole. Her pulse pounded in her ears. Could Archie hear it too?

"I know you are in here." He frowned as he pointed his flashlight at the corners of the room. She pulled her feet in behind the boxes. The toe of her left sneaker stuck out a little, but she couldn't pull it back any farther. She pushed against the boxes to make more room, but the top one crashed to the ground.

Archie spun around and shone his light on the corner.

"Got you." He chuckled.

Sam froze. Her heart was pounding right out of her chest. She clenched her teeth to stop from running away screaming at the top of her lungs.

"I heard a crash." Red jogged into the room and right into Archie, who dropped his flashlight.

This was her chance. She jetted out of her hiding spot, around the boxes, and into the next room. She pulled a dusty tarp over her head.

"My light." Archie's voice was muted.

The two men scuffled. She pressed her clammy palms over her chest. She had to get away. She crawled to a corner and under some doors leaning against the wall. She pressed one hand to her chest and one over her mouth.

"You moron." Archie slammed something against the wall.

Sam peeked through a crack. Archie snatched the flashlight off the floor. Time stood still, as Archie pointed the light where she hid, then moved it around the room.

"I had her."

"Jim," Red called. "Archie found the girl."

Sam pressed her fist to her chest. Why weren't Red and Archie leaving? Big Jim would be here soon, and she'd really be in trouble. She inched along the wall and sank behind another dusty support beam as Big Jim walked into the room. She pressed against the wall. Sam peered through a crack in the wall. Who was this guy who sounded so much like Dad? She pulled back. His eyes were hazel just like Dad's.

"Archie." Big Jim reached a hand down to help Archie stand. "You're here to help us. Remember?"

No. This couldn't be Dad. How could he know Archie or Red? And where did he get those clothes? They were shapeless and odd faded colors. They were just like Henri's. Besides, Big Jim had stubble, and Dad always shaved.

"You two idiots have no idea who I am." Archie

swung at Red who held him at arm's length.

Why was Archie so angry? Should she find a new hiding place? Why did they need to find her? Well, besides the fact that she was lost. She didn't trust Archie, and she didn't know if Red was really Henri's dad. She had no choice but to wait until they left.

"Aren't you two forgetting about Stickel?" Archie asked.

Stickel? Every muscle in her body tightened. Mr. Stickel was key to whatever was going on here and in 1901. Plus, she had Henri's dad in her vision. How was she ever going to get him back to 1901 like she promised?

"That's the only reason you're here, Archie." Big Jim walked over to Archie who shrank the closer he got. "The Secret Service needs your information about Stickel."

"What are you talking about?" Archie squirmed in Red's grasp.

Sam sat fascinated by the scene playing out in the next room. Red and Big Jim had the upper hand, no matter what Archie's connection was to Mr. Stickel. And what did Big Jim mean by Secret Service agents?

"You worked for him, right?" Big Jim asked. "But we can't stop Stickel until we find those girls."

"Nicole," Sam murmured and clamped her hand over her mouth. Her heart raced as she squeezed farther into her corner, cobwebs clinging to her arms and hair.

"Fine. What do you need me to do?" Archie yawned.

"Cooperate like you agreed." Red shook Archie by the collar.

Sinking back into the corner, Sam couldn't believe what she was hearing. How had her plan to get Dad back gotten so crazy, and how was Henri's dad going to get back to 1901, and how was Nicole going to get back to the present? What a mess.

Big Jim glared from Archie to Red. "Once we have the girls, we can track down Stickel and arrest him for embezzlement."

"Mr. Stickel will not be so easy to find." Archie wiped his nose on his shoulder. "You know those girls were never part of his plan. What if he finds them first?"

"You leave Stickel to me." Big Jim pointed a finger at Archie. "Find that girl. She doesn't know these tunnels, right?"

The hair on her arms stood on end.

"This way." Jim stormed out of the room, and Red, holding Archie by the arm, shuffled after him.

Sam sighed and scratched her head. What did they mean by the plan for Mr. Stickel? Didn't Archie say he disappeared? But they never found his body, or Big Jim's, or Red's, and here they were all alive.

"None of those tour stories were true." Sam sighed and buried her face in her hands.

Chapter 6

One Week Earlier

The moon hung in the midnight sky, as Jim Stewart knocked on the door at house number 377.

"Figures." He wiped his eyes with a handkerchief and blew his nose. "This always happens during a full moon."

He stood on the cement steps the porch light illuminating the white window frames, a stark contrast to the red brick walls that rose into the dark night. Why had he walked out? Because Sam couldn't know about the bricks, not yet. She was too young to take on the role of protector, and he wanted to shield her from the family curse for as long as he could. Yet, she grew more suspicious each time he was called away. How long could this go on without her figuring it out?

"It's unlocked," a weak voice called. "Come in."

Of course, it was unlocked. What did she have to fear? He opened the door, the scent of lavender enveloping him. She used the same fragrance on her cards and the notepaper. Why did everything have to be such a secret? He was tired of keeping secrets, but Sam's safety depended on it. He gritted his teeth as he stepped into the entry, resenting the woman who called him to action.

Carol's safety depended on secrecy too. His chest

ached with this forced deception. He'd never lied to her in the eighteen years they'd been married, or to Sam, but the Roman Bricks and lavender notes…

He gazed at the fire casting a yellow glow on Aunt Eli sitting in her chair. Her ginger cat lay curled in a ball in front of the fire. Aunt Eli gave him his missions, and if he wanted his life back and his family safe, he'd do his job and follow her instructions. As the protector, he had no choice.

He hung his coat on a hook in the entry before striding into the living room. Aunt Eli sat dwarfed by the overstuffed chair, a purple afghan across her lap.

He crossed the room in four steps and bent to kiss the cheek she offered. "Good evening, Aunt," James said.

With shaking hands, she pushed on the armrests trying to stand. He put a hand on her shoulder, and she clasped his hand with her gnarled fingers. The Family Bible lay open in her lap and a shiver shook his tall frame.

"They're disappearing, you know." She ran her hand over the pages of the family tree.

Her words left him hollow, and his heart began to race. "Does that mean?" His throat went dry.

"Yes. Someone has used the bricks." She gazed up at him, her pale blue eyes steady. Her face sagged with ninety-two years of holding secrets.

Was she crying? James blinked. The only time Aunt Eli had ever cried was at Grandmother's funeral. His stomach cramped and he sank into a matching overstuffed chair.

"You said they were disappearing? Whose so far?" James knew he wouldn't like the answer.

"Mine is faded, which is no surprise, your mother's is fading, but Sam's is almost gone. You know what this means."

"Someone has used the bricks and created a fault in the space-time continuum." A tremble ran through his body like a wave. Who would do such a thing? He'd inherited this job from his father, but it never got easier, and this was the worst case so far. "Who would be so reckless?"

"Only one person."

He clenched his fists and stood at attention before Aunt Eli. She gazed up at him, weeping. The flickering flames gleamed off her cheeks, or were they flickering through her? Was she growing transparent?

"This is even worse than the 1961 disaster." He glanced at Aunt Eli. They'd never found the girl, but that was before his time. It was the first example of what could go wrong that his father had ever shared with him.

Aunt Eli wouldn't send him on this mission if she didn't have to. She wouldn't break her own heart again, not at her age. He pulled his chair closer, and she turned to the last pages of the Bible.

"I have everything we need. Here's the key, and here are the words of the spell they used." Aunt Eli unfolded a lavender piece of paper. "The Duke must go with you." The ginger cat raised his head and gave a silent meow.

Jim frowned at the cat. "Archibald? Why?"

"You know why. This started in Portland, and his connection to the bricks will aid in your success."

He trusted her, but not Archie. If the names were disappearing, though, it made sense that The Duke would go.

"This is the only way." She nodded, and as she read

the spell, the room began to shake. The ginger cat jumped to its feet. James inhaled and counted to ten. He had to stay sharp and do whatever it took to save his family. Sam's life depended on it.

Chapter 7

The Sailor Suit

Nicole stared at Yabuki Laundry carved in a board hung over the door. What had she expected? Not this. Clotheslines hung crisscrossed from wall to wall at one end of the room, hiding her from the workers. Shirts, pants, and towels hung on the lines like shriveled fruit. Peering through the hanging sheets, she scanned the room but couldn't make sense of the scene in front of her.

A woman stood to stretch her back. Henri slipped behind the sheet. Nicole scanned the room, but the woman didn't notice Henri or her. She counted five women in all. Where were the machines? The woman stuck her hands back into a tub with gray water. Nicole would never complain about picking up her dirty clothes again.

The laundry workroom was on the tunnel level. Henri crouched along a wall and stopped at a little room in the back. A girl with black hair pulled into a long braid sat at a table behind a row of bed sheets hanging on a line. She sorted clothes from baskets that had tags on them with names like Webster and Brady. The customers. Footsteps clomped on the floor of the shop above as Henri led her to the girl.

"Did Paul deliver my message?" Henri asked.

"Yes. He just left." Misa stood and made a slight bow. "You are Nickle."

"It's pronounced Ni-coal." She stuck out her hand. Misa stared at it, looked up, and grinned with perfect, white teeth. Nicole sighed, and the tension in her neck and shoulders melted away. Misa's dark eyes were a gentle brown, and Nicole nodded, needing a friend right now.

Henri nodded. "Right. I must get back to the Lucky Star. Misa will find clothing for you. Then you must return to the stockroom."

Was Henri leaving her alone here? She held out her hand to stop her, but Henri turned and disappeared under a sheet. Nicole opened her mouth to object, but she was gone. Misa took her arm and led her to a sink with a window above that stood open. The air was fresh and cooler here. Misa handed her a cloth.

"You should wash. You will feel better."

Nicole turned to say thanks, but Misa had disappeared behind a sheet. A shaky sigh escaped her as she rinsed her hands and face with warm water. Everyone was disappearing, Sam, Henri, now Misa. She stood alone at the sink, scrubbing her mind a whirl of questions. Was Sam okay? Had she gone to Seattle? Would she come back?

Misa brushed under the sheet. "I found this."

"Oh." Nicole dropped the towel and took a step back. The thick pile of clothes had a clean, musky odor.

Misa held out a white shirt and pants with brass buttons and red and blue trim. Was that a sailor suit? Misa laid the white shirt over the back of a chair near the sink and bowed, a smile turning up the corner of her mouth.

Where were the brown pants? Where was the gray shirt like Henri's? Nicole stared at the clothes. "Thanks?" She lifted the towel from the floor and draped it on the edge of the sink. She forced a smile to her lips as she lifted the shirt. It was a sailor suit.

She lifted the pants. "Oh, and matching shorts." The wool shorts were even heavier than the shirt and sweat trickled down her back. She couldn't wear this, not in July. At least people in 1901 didn't have cameras.

"These clothes are much nicer than those I found for Henri." Misa smiled and bowed again.

Nicole sighed. She'd wear a suit of armor if it helped her get home. She stepped out of her jeans and into the wool shorts. They hung around her waist.

Misa handed her a pair of red suspenders. "This will keep your trousers from falling down."

Nicole shook her head. Could this outfit get any better? Had Sam set this up? Misa buttoned the suspenders to the back of the shorts and watched as Nicole buttoned the front.

She didn't want to appear ungrateful, but this outfit was ridiculous. She pulled the heavy wool shirt over her head. Misa smiled at her, waiting. Was there no such thing as privacy in 1901, or maybe it was just the Yabuki Laundry and the whole borrowing clothes thing? Her knobby knees wobbled. Misa was a friend, right? Someone to help her. Nicole patted Misa's hand and sank into the wooden chair by the sink.

"You came through the bricks." Misa pulled a towel from the clothesline and folded it.

Had someone used the bricks? Misa laid the towel on a table and reached for another one. How did Misa stay so calm? The air grew hotter.

"What do you know about the bricks?" Nicole tried to smile. Could she really trust Misa? Clearing her throat, she flipped up the collar, then flipped it down. Was that normal behavior in 1901 when someone was wearing a sailor suit, discussing magic bricks? Probably not.

"Frederick explained the bricks to me." Misa looked down as she said this, and her cheeks turn pink. Misa folded another towel and placed it on the small table.

"Frederick? Who is—"

"A friend." Misa's eyelashes fluttered.

So far no one had used a first name in 1901. Frederick must be close to her somehow, maybe a boyfriend?

"You are lucky to be alive. The bricks are fickle and inconsistent at best."

"What?" Nicole stared at Misa. These bricks were a surprise a minute. What else did Misa know? Nicole perched on the edge of the chair. "So, what about Sam?"

"You are stuck in this time, just as Sam is stuck in yours, but only for the moment."

Misa's story was better suited to a crypt than a small room at the back of a washroom. The hair on the back of her neck stood on end.

"S-s-so, people use these bricks on a regular basis, like...all the time?" She waited, her pulse pounding in her ears. Had she really been excited to go on that OPU tour? She'd wanted to explore history and the underground and hear the stories, but she didn't want to visit or become part of history. How was this even happening?

Misa sighed. "Frederick took me to the Lucky Star Saloon. I have seen the bricks." She wore the same serene look on her face, as though she were talking about the next basket of clothes she had to fold.

"Did you use them?"

"No. Frederick and Elise Meyer brought them to life for Mr. Stickel."

"Brought them to life?" Nicole stood. How could bricks come alive?

Misa continued, as though Nicole hadn't interrupted her. "So, he could go to Nome, Alaska for the gold rush."

"Nome, Alas—?" She shivered as a drop of sweat ran down her spine. The harsh soap burned her eyes. Was that why they watered? She hadn't read this in any of the stories she'd found on the underground tour. What else did Misa know? Was she changing history?

Her hands shook, and she choked out, "Did Sam go to Alaska?"

"No." Misa's eyes gleamed in the candlelight as she told Nicole the story. "Frederick said that Mr. Stickel plans to steal money from his own bank then change his name and disappear in the throngs going to Alaska."

"The bank that was never robbed." Nicole paced in a circle. This was starting to make sense. "He never succeeded."

"I do not know beyond what Frederick told me." Misa stood with her hands clasped in front of her in her sleeves as though she didn't even have hands.

A shiver ran through her. Nicole and Sam were not just traveling through time. They were smack in the middle of a crime that was taking place at this very minute. They had to stop it.

"Did you tell this to Sam?" Nicole lifted the red bow and with shaking fingers attempted to tie it around her neck. Misa grabbed the material and tied it brushing the bow gently against her throat. How could she remain so calm? What wasn't she saying?

"Henri wants to find her father. She cares about nothing else. However, I saw her father, Mr. McClusky, chasing Mr. Stickel, and he was with another man. I will tell her when the time is right."

She was withholding information, but why wouldn't she just tell Henri? Nicole sobbed and wiped her face with shaky hands. "I wish Sam knew this. It could save her life, if she's in Seattle, that is." Why did Sam have to touch those bricks?

"Hush," Misa whispered. "Do you want to be found?"

"Found?" Was that an option? "What does that mean, found?"

"I am supposed to be working alone today. If someone hears your voice. Well..."

Nicole held out her hand and Misa took it. "Tell me."

"You must realize that women disappear in these tunnels almost as often as men do."

"They get shanghaied too?" The room grew warm again. Would she ever survive this?

"Shanghaied, you know. Or maybe you don't." Nicole pursed her lips. "I think Henri called it Crimper?"

"Yes, I understand crimper. Mr. Lawrence is a crimper, but he not only crimps men to work on ships. He crimps women as well. My older sister, Akemi, has been missing for six months, ever since she delivered laundry to Mr. Lawrence at the saloon."

"The Lucky Dog?"

"Lucky Star. Mr. Lawrence must have offered her a drink, and it was most likely drugged. That's how they get the men. When Akemi lost consciousness, we believe they put her on a ship headed out to sea because we never heard from her again."

"No way. Why did Mr. Lawrence do that?" Nicole shivered and wrapped her arms around her wool-clad torso. She gave her head a shake. Misa's story was something out of a nightmare.

"Akemi told me she saw Mr. Stickel use the bricks. It was an accident." Misa hung her head. "It should have been me. It was my day to deliver, but Akemi went. Mr. Stickel must have found out, and. . ." Misa wiped a tear from her cheek. "I've heard of other women taken in these tunnels. It is horrible. . ."

"But why?" Nicole whispered. "What kind of place is this?"

"A dangerous place, if you are not careful."

"Then why are you here?"

"I live here with my father and work here with my family." She swung her hand to indicate the people at the washtubs. "I don't have to leave *Nihon Machi* except through the tunnels"

"Nihon-what?"

"Japan Town. I was born in Portland, but it is dangerous for me to leave *Nihon Machi*. People don't like the Japanese here."

"Well, that's racist, isn't it?" Nicole couldn't process what Misa was telling her. Where was Sam? Nothing Misa said made sense to her.

"I do not know this word, rah-sit." Misa folded a sheet and stacked it on the table next to the towels. Was this just another day in her life?

Nicole adjusted the suspenders that held her heavy wool shorts from falling. She struggled to find the words to define racist. Misa stared at her with a gaze she might have if the sky were always blue and birds were always singing, and she wasn't stuck in this muggy underground laundry in a conversation with a girl from the future about racism and women being sold into slavery.

Nicole shook her head. "None of this can be true."

"I speak only what I know to be true." Misa shrugged. "You are ready now. You must go." She grabbed a lantern that sat on the table. The flame waivered as Misa led her along the back wall to the entrance of the tunnel.

Could she trust what Misa had just told her? It was all consistent with the stories she'd read and with everything that had happened so far. She couldn't afford not to trust Misa.

Misa pulled back a curtain. "Henri will meet you in the room with the bricks."

Tears threatened to spill from her eyes, and she swallowed hard. "How will I find my way?" Would Misa offer to go with her if she cried?

"Look for this mark." Misa held up the lantern and pointed to a stick man holding a flag. "This symbol will lead you to the Lucky Star storeroom. It is not far. I promise."

"I don't know…" She glanced at the image then back at Misa who handed her the lantern. She couldn't lift her arm or move her feet. How would she walk?

"You must help Sam decipher the magic of the bricks. Sam must be here to break their spell and stop them from being used for evil. I realize that now." Misa bowed.

Nicole opened her mouth to speak, but the words wouldn't come. Was Misa a seer? Was she dangerous too? She took the lantern, and Misa disappeared through the sheets hanging like ghosts across the room.

Nicole glared at the stickman figure carved into the doorframe, and bracing her shoulders, she stepped into the dark tunnel.

Chapter 8

When One Door Closes—

Nicole scanned the storeroom of the Lucky Star Saloon. Same crates, same barrels. The stickmen worked like Misa said, but where was Henri?

Holding out the lantern, she searched behind barrels of whiskey and boxes filled with bottles stacked against one wall. The space wasn't that large. Where could she be? Flour, salt, and large pots and pans were all she found. Her knees wobbled, as she resisted the urge to crawl into a corner and hide.

She cupped a hand to her ear. Were those footsteps? They were, and they were getting louder. She turned her lantern off and crouched behind a barrel. A beam of light filled the stockroom, and Henri came into view.

Nicole stood, her heart pounding. "You could have called out or something? I thought I was going to have a heart attack."

"A heart what?"

Nicole placed a hand over her heart.

"I see. I apologize, but still, you must keep your voice down." Henri pointed to the floor over their heads and frowned at her. "Mr. Lawrence is in the saloon, and he is angry. He lectured me on my tasks and completing them in a timely manner."

"I never want to meet Hairy Larry." Nicole leaned

against a barrel. The mention of his name made her pause.

"I must go. He awaits his keg of salt."

"No. Don't leave me again." Was the room growing warm, or was it just the sailor suit? Was she allergic to wool? She fanned her face.

"I must go, but I'll return soon." Henri walked to the shelves and pulled off a small wooden box with SALT stenciled on the side. She set it next to the lantern on the barrel and shuffled her feet, hesitating.

Did she have something on her mind? "What's up?"

Henri glanced at the ceiling. "What is up? Is something up there?"

"It means is something wrong?" Was she going to have to explain everything she said?

"Maybe. You were right. Mr. Stickel is back in 1901, and he wants Hairy Larry to put a man in this room to guard the bricks, which would be problematic for Sam if she returns."

"That would be a problem." She paced in a circle. If the room had a guard, she might never see Sam again or get back home. "So, what can we do? What if Sam comes back?" She pulled on her collar to let in some cool air, the heavy fabric clinging to her sweaty back. At least she wasn't in pants sweating even worse.

"We can only hope Sam stays in Seattle where she belongs." Henri shrugged her shoulders. "Assuming she did go to Seattle and back to your time. It's hard to know where she is, isn't it?"

"Of course, she's in Seattle. Where else would she go? Don't say things like that." She pressed a hand to her chest as she struggled to control her breathing. Her heart raced as if she'd been running through the tunnels. When would this roller coaster of emotions end?

"Maybe Misa has an idea. She seems to know a lot about those bricks." Nicole frowned. "She told me that I was here to help Sam figure out how the magic works. Do you know what that means?"

"I do not, but somehow you arrived in this place. That cannot be a coincidence, can it?"

"I still don't get it." She stood with her hands on her hips, the wool hot and itchy. She wanted her clothes back. She wanted her home and her room with her phone, her games, and her friends. But she knew she wasn't going anywhere until Sam either returned or she figured out how to use the bricks herself.

"What I meant was you were in Seattle in your time this morning, but this afternoon you find yourself in Portland in 1901. I do not know why it was you and Sam, but it was, so there must be a reason, right?" Henri gazed at her with clear blue eyes.

"I suppose, but Misa said the bricks were magic." She sighed. Her head ached from thinking so hard. "I don't know magic, and neither does Sam. All she did was touch those stupid bricks and we were in the Lucky Star stockroom. Now, look at me. I'm in this stupid sailor suit. My mom is going to ground me for the rest of my life." She sank onto a crate and bent at the waist, burying her head in her arms.

"I do not understand your meaning of ground in this context, but I do know that we can solve this problem. We just need to think of a solution together. Let us go over what we know." Henri put a hand on Nicole's arm. Nicole lifted her head and nodded.

Henri paced. "Mr. Lawrence is in charge of the Lucky Star Saloon, and the Roman Bricks are under that

71

saloon, so that is one link to Mr. Stickel. We know for that certain."

"Okay, so Mr. Stickel is not dead, and Mr. Lawrence is somehow involved. Your dad might be involved too, and you might be in danger."

"Why would I be in danger?" Henri asked. She scratched her head. "Do you think my papa is in the future? This might be good news. I would rather he was in the future than shanghaied and far out to sea."

"That might be better, but Mr. Lawrence is still here. Your knowledge of these tunnels could save our lives, especially if we have to run."

"Run?" Henri frowned.

"Hairy Larry is mad, right? You said so yourself."

"Yes, but..." Henri stopped talking and pointed at a spot on the wall. "Look."

The bricks glowed on the wall.

****

The dust rose as Sam inched across the floor on her hands and knees, little pieces of gravel digging into her palms. She clenched her teeth and cleared her throat. The heavy odor of damp wood and an eon of dust filled her senses. She had to find a way out of the underground. Then what? Go home? Find the police? Who could she tell about this? Who would believe her and help her get Nicole back to the present?

She put a hand over her mouth to stifle a cough as she leaned forward and peeked around the corner. Big Jim and Red were somewhere down here, and she had to get to the bricks without being seen. The only way to help Nicole was to go back to 1901, but would the bricks work?

She crawled around a door leaning against the wall.

She spotted the bricks, but something was different. Their edges looked fuzzy as they expanded and contracted. A humming vibrated through the air. Did something move? She moved toward the bricks, but she stopped. She scanned the room. An orange tabby lay on a crate against the wall the Roman bricks were on. It licked its paws and washed its face like nothing was wrong. It must live here. Was it guarding the bricks? It lifted its head and stared at her with amber eyes.

"Pft." She shook her head. This cat wasn't guarding the bricks. She moved to the cat. It rolled onto its back exposing a furry, orange belly.

"You softie. You couldn't guard cupcakes. Where did you come from? You're too clean to live here." The cat purred and reached up a paw as if to grab her. She chuckled and ran her fingers through the cat's silky fur. It had a white chest and white paws, so familiar like—

Wait. Aunt Eli's cat? "Duke?"

She placed her palm on the cat's warm soft belly and closed her eyes. The soft purring vibrated against her hand, and she sighed. This couldn't be Sir Archibald, the Duke of Pisica could it? Home. She felt so close, but she couldn't be sure if this was her present or 1901.

Besides, she couldn't go home without Nicole. Was she still in the Lucky Star stockroom? She must be terrified. Sam gripped a board in the wall and stared at the bricks. She had to go back. With a sigh, she climbed onto the crate. The cat watched her as she reached up. A breeze blew across her face, and she closed her eyes.

"Wha—"

Sam hit the floor. She opened her eyes, and Nicole lay sprawled on top of her. The cat leapt off the crate, arching its back.

Sam lifted her head. "Nicole?"

"Sam?" Nicole crawled off of Sam, her eyes glassy, her square collar standing up against the back of her head like a sail. She touched her ankle and pulled her hand away. "Oh no. I think it's sprained."

"Is it really you?" Sam clasped Nicole in a hug, then held her at arm's length. "I can't believe you made it back." She glanced into the darkness for Red and Big Jim. Had they heard her? Dust rose from the floor and hung in the silence. Sam wiped her nose. She glanced at the bricks which no longer glowed.

Nicole rubbed her ankle. "Is that a cat?"

The cat stretched and yawned then trotted out of the room.

"It is." Sam put a hand over her mouth as the square collar fell back across Nicole's shoulders as she grunted to a stand. "What are you wearing?" Sam bit her lip to stop a grin.

Nicole glared at her. "It's not funny." She brushed dust off her shorts and adjusted her collar. "It's all Misa could find in my size."

"It's kind of funny." Sam shook her head. "But the important thing is you're here, and we can go home now."

She stood but held up a hand. Footsteps were coming. She grabbed Nicole's hand. Was there time? She gazed up at the dull bricks.

Big Jim appeared in the doorway. He blocked their only way out, but he didn't move toward them. Sam couldn't make out his facial features, but there was something about him. She stared, waiting for him to call Red, but he didn't. He took a couple of steps into the room, and pulling his hat off, he ran his hand over his hair. She shivered. Dad?

No. Dad would have said something, right? Big Jim had moved out of the doorway. She glanced at Nicole. Nicole nodded, and gripping her hand, Sam ran past Big Jim.

Racing down an uneven path, dust tickled her nose and she pinched back a sneeze. Nicole hobbled and skipped along behind her. Sam ducked into another shadow-filled room. Nicole plopped down next to her and rubbed her ankle. "Oh, man."

"Are you all right?"

"I can't put weight on it." Nicole looked up at Sam, her face pinched with pain.

How would they escape if Nicole couldn't run?

"Was that Big Jim?"

Sam's stomach did a flip. "Yes. Red is here too." Did Nicole notice Big Jim's resemblance to Dad?

"Did you see how he moved to the side? It was like he wanted us to get away." Nicole rubbed her ankle. "What year is this?"

Sam scratched her head. She knelt beside Nicole. "I don't know. We'd have to go out of the underground to figure that out, but Big Jim and Red have blocked our escape."

"I can't run anyway. I'm not going to make it, Sam." Nicole cradled her ankle, tears running down her face.

"What? Yes, you are. We're together and we're getting out of here." She stood, and grabbing Nicole's hand, they dash-hopped across the hall and into a space under some stairs, a tall, wide Shipley's Shaving Cream sign leaned against the stairs and hid them.

"Shhh. They're coming."

"What if they find us?" Nicole stared at Sam with

tear-filled eyes.

Sam shrugged. "Big Jim hesitated long enough for us to escape. We can't waste that opportunity." What was she saying? She clamped a hand over her mouth as Big Jim and Red ran right past them and down the hall. Was Big Jim leading Red away from them?

Nicole's lips were pressed into a thin line. She wiped her eyes. "Why are Red and Big Jim after us?" Nicole paused. "Their clothes are old-fashioned like Henri's, and—"

"Wait. They look like Archie's, too."

"That's it." Sam stared at Nicole. "Archie must be from 1901, too. Come on."

"How can Archie be from 1901?"

She pulled Nicole to a stand and helped her hobble down the wood-framed hallway. The dust rose and made her cough. She stopped. "Wait. We have to get back to the bricks."

Nicole gripped Sam's hand as they retraced their steps and entered the room with the bare lightbulb.

Nicole scanned the wall. "I don't see them glowing anymore."

"There they are." Sam pointed. "They aren't glowing, but they might still work." Sam glanced at Nicole.

"Quick. Touch them." Nicole held her sprained ankle off the floor.

"Shhh." Sam spun around.

Someone was running back toward them. Nicole's face went white.

"They must have snuck by us." Big Jim's voice boomed down the hallway. He was running toward Sam and Nicole, and he wasn't alone.

"Sam, quick." Nicole nudged Sam.

She grabbed Nicole's hand, tugged her onto the crate, and reaching up, Nicole slapped her hand on the bricks. "Nothing's happening." Nicole slapped the bricks over and over. "Work, you stupid bricks."

"They're at the bricks, quickly." Red's voice echoed in the underground.

"Why aren't they working?" Sam jumped off the crate, and hauling Nicole's arm across her shoulder, they hobbled to the far corner of the room. A sheet of plywood leaned against the wall. With her free hand, Sam pulled it back to reveal a closet-sized space. "In here."

"No." Nicole pulled back. "Spiders."

"What?" Sam pulled Nicole into the space behind the plywood. It knocked against the wall, and Sam stopped, holding a finger to her lips. Did they hear that? She peered between a crack in the boards. Light from the bare bulb in the hallway filtered through the wall. She gasped as Big Jim and Red rushed into the room.

"Did they use the bricks?" Big Jim ran to the bricks that still glowed on the wall.

"How would we know?" Red paced the room, as Sam watched, one hand over her mouth, the other clutching Nicole's.

"These damnable bricks complicate everything. I had no idea the Secret Service had such weapons, and where is Archie?"

Red thought the bricks were a weapon? Were they?

Big Jim rubbed his face. "Archie is an informant, but he works for Stickel, remember? He has his own agenda."

Was he nervous? Sam glanced at Nicole. Her eyes reflected the light that seeped into the room from the bulb in the hall.

"Did he say informant?" Nicole squeezed Sam's hand, and she squeezed back.

Red pressed his palm to the bricks. His auburn hair was cut short, but it still curled at the temples, like Henri's. Both men wore shapeless wool jackets and slacks with black boots. Sweat dripped down Big Jim's cheek. Were these the bank robbers from Archie's story or agents working a case? And why were they looking for her and not Mr. Stickel? A shiver ran through her. Red was Henri's dad, but who was Big Jim?

"Argh." Red slapped the bricks.

"Red," Big Jim said. "They might not have used the bricks."

"Sorry. You are right, Jim. It is just that I have a daughter the same age as those girls, and I'd hate to see anything bad happen to them."

"Bad?" Nicole gripped Sam's hand.

"Shh." Sam pulled Nicole's hand to her chest. She shook her head and Nicole nodded.

"I do too, buddy." Big Jim put a hand on Red's shoulder.

"I've never seen anyone as desperate as Mr. Stickel, but we will catch him."

"First, we must find those girls. We can't arrest Stickel until we know they're safe." Big Jim frowned.

The bricks glowed on the wall. She needed to get close enough to use them, but how? She had to get to Henri, let her know her dad was alive.

"Where is Archie?" Red glared at the bricks.

Sam glanced at Nicole who mouthed, "Tour-guide-Archie?' She held a finger to her lips. How was Archie involved? Where was Mr. Stickel?

"He's not in here, and neither are the girls. We better check the other rooms." Big Jim turned and Red followed him out of the room and down the hallway.

"So, Archie and Mr. Stickel are here?" Nicole's soft voice shook.

"I don't know." Sam ran her fingers over her arm, dust clinging to them.

Nicole's voice hissed into the darkness. "So, what's our plan? Can we go home now?"

"Home?" She gazed into Nicole's eyes. "Henri still needs our help. Red is her dad, and he's here. We can't go home until we figure out how to get him back to Henri. The bricks are the answer, but how?"

"Wait. Red is Henri's dad?" Nicole paused. "This is that Red?"

"How many Reds are there? They must have used the bricks too, and somehow, they know we did."

Nicole sank against the wall in the dark space rubbing her ankle. "Why did you have to touch them?"

"Uh." She reached into her pocket and rolled the key in her fingers. Why had she touched the bricks? How did she tell Nicole that they had called to her, and now she had to help get Red back to Henri?

"Hey, I have bars." Nicole stared at her phone. "I'm calling home."

"What?"

"I'm calling my mom."

Sam grabbed Nicole's phone. "Not until we solve the mystery of these bricks, and everyone is in their right time." She scanned the wall. The bricks glowed, mesmerizing her. "We have to go back to 1901."

She handed Nicole her phone and squeezed from behind the sheet of plywood. Nicole limped behind her, and she helped Nicole climb onto a crate under the bricks. She stood beside Nicole and reached for the bricks as someone entered the room. Nicole gasped. The silhouette of a man blocked the doorway.

Chapter 9

Mr. Lawrence

Nicole held her hand over the bricks, and Sam kept her gaze on the fat old man in top hat and jacket. He reminded Sam of the banker on Monopoly with his big round belly straining the buttons of his white shirt. He stood with his hands on his knees, huffing and puffing.

"You girls are going to be the death of me," the man said between gasps. "So maybe I'll return the favor."

"Who are you?" Sam stood on the crate by Nicole ready to slap the bricks if he got too close.

"I am Mr. Charles Mortimer Stickel, Esq."

Sam gasped.

"Mr. Stickel?" Nicole squeaked.

"I'm supposed to be catching the S.S. Portland, a steamer heading to Alaska today—" He stopped and glared at them. "—in 1901, but when you touched those bricks, I ended up here in the future." He shook his fist at them. "You have spoiled my beautiful plan, girls, and now you will pay." He chuckled a deep ho-ho-ho, like an evil-Santa. He looked like one, short and round, if Santa ever wore a tuxedo and top hat.

Sam trembled. "You're mad?"

"What are you two waiting for, an invitation? Climb down from there at once."

"Quick, Sam. A little help." Nicole's hand rested on

the bricks.

"Right." Sam slapped her own hand over Nicole's, and the air made a familiar sucking sound, and her ears rang.

Dust rose from the crate where the girls had once stood. Mr. Stickel clawed at the air. "No, no, no."

He stared at the bricks glowing on the wall. "Drat those pesky girls."

Footsteps pounded down the hall getting closer. He folded his fingers and cracked his knuckles. Then rubbing his hands together, he stepped onto the crate and placed both of his hands on the Roman bricks. Closing his eyes, he recited some words.

Big Jim raced into the room as Mr. Stickel disappeared.

"How does he do that?" Red glared at the spot on the crate that had held Mr. Stickel. He scratched his head.

Jim shrugged. How many times would he have to lie? Probably as many times as he had to travel through these darned bricks. "All I know is that he's dangerous, and we have to apprehend him. That's why D.C. sent me."

"Right." Red frowned.

"What do we know?" Jim tried a basic question. Maybe that would get Red's mind off the bricks.

Red shook his head, his gaze on the bricks. "He was mumbling something, like a spell."

"That must be how he makes the bricks work." Big Jim put his face inches from the bricks and examined them. "Did you catch what he said before he touched the bricks?" Aunt Eli was right. Someone had used the bricks. Stickel. Now he had to learn the circumstances. Only then could he stop the names from disappearing.

Well, that and he had to reintroduce Red to his great-great-grandmother so they could fall in love, get married, and stop the names from disappearing. Easy. Jim raked his fingers through his hair.

Red's brows furrowed. "I think he said something about ancestors, pleas, and portals?"

Jim nodded. Aunt Eli's instructions were clear. To stop the names from disappearing, he had to stop Stickel and get his great, greats to meet, fall in love, etcetera, etcetera. He held a hand to his head. What would he do if a real Secret Service Agent from D.C. showed up? He'd better be back in the present by the time that happened.

"I heard something about bended knee and loving plea, but what was the part about portals? My guess is that whatever he said has to be repeated with exact precision or the bricks won't work."

"Stickel's assistant might know, especially if he's using the bricks too." Red stood to his full height of six foot, three inches and peered into the underground. "Archie."

****

Sam landed on her bottom. She held her head in her hands. Nicole wobbled and put a hand on the floor to steady herself as she sat on the floor and took in her surroundings.

"Barrels and crates with Lucky Star stenciled on them. We're in 1901 again." Sam jumped to her feet. Her heart raced as though she'd been running. It had raced every time. Who knew time-travel was so strenuous?

"We escaped Mr. Stickel." She brushed off her pants.

"Yes," Nicole rubbed her ankle. "But how? Why

don't those bricks work all the time?"

"I have no clue, but I when I put my hand on yours, they did, and lucky for us. Mr. Stickel isn't here." Sam helped Nicole to stand. "How's your ankle?"

"We have bigger problems than my ankle. If Mr. Stickel knows we're back in 1901, he's going to follow us if he can get the bricks to work."

"How? I mean, I'm the one who makes them work, but I don't know how."

"Well, I got them to work—once." Nicole placed her hands on her hips. "Which raises the question. Why did you leave me in 1901?"

"What? That was part of the plan, remember?" Sam had to find Henri, but Nicole's glare stopped her. How did she distract her this time? "Misa gave you boy's clothes."

"She did." Nicole shrugged. "I also learned some interesting facts from her. She told me about some guy named Frederick and the bricks, and did you know Misa's sister disappeared?"

"Disappeared?" Was this the same as the names disappearing? She glanced at Nicole who folded her arms across her chest and glared. "But—"

A loud thump filled the room, and dust rose. She coughed, fanning the air with her hand. A figure sat on the ground. A man. "Mr. Stickel?"

"You girls are trespassing. This is private property."

Sam shuddered.

Mr. Stickel pushed himself off the ground and brushed off his slacks. A film of grime clung to his sweaty face.

Sam reeled several steps back as he walked toward her.

"No, no, no." Sam pulled Nicole with her, and they scurried toward the door. She skidded to a stop, but Nicole stumbled against her. She put up her hand to stop herself.

A tall man with a tangle of dark hair blocked their only means of escape.

Mr. Stickel chuckled and rubbed his hands together. "Why, Lawrence. Your timing is perfect."

"Mr. Lawrence?" Sam whispered and clung to Nicole. Sam stared at the tall man in the doorway. His cold eyes bore into her like ice. Why was Mr. Stickel grinning? Sam shivered. How would she get them out of this mess?

"Sir?" Mr. Lawrence's voice rumbled in his chest, and the timbers that held up the walls seemed to shake, but that was impossible, right?

"Hairy Larry?" Nicole gasped. "I never wanted to meet him, remember?" She cowered against the wall.

Mr. Lawrence stooped to glare at both girls. "Do not call me by that rude and hurtful name." He frowned; his raven brows bunched over his eyes.

Sam shrank beside Nicole. Mr. Lawrence's black beard was trimmed and neat, but the hair on his head sprang out in a mass of coils. Black hairs pushed up through his collar. Henri had not exaggerated. He was hairy and large. She didn't want to make him angry. Was it too late for that?

"Show these girls to their room." Mr. Stickel giggled in an evil-Santa way.

Sam shivered and her legs turned to mush. Their room? They didn't have a room, and she didn't want to go anywhere with Mr. Lawrence. She needed a plan, but what should she do in the meantime? She glanced at

Nicole, her face the color of her white collar.

"Walk this way, girls."

Hairy Larry grabbed Sam by the arm and dragged her down the tunnel. He can't touch me. Why did he touch me? She shuffled down the hall, Nicole clutching the back of her shirt. Mr. Lawrence pulled her forward, and she hustled to keep up with him, Nicole hobbling on her sprained ankle. Mr. Stickel's footsteps echoed off the walls as he followed.

This corridor was darker than the ones Henri had taken them through. A lump formed in Sam's throat. Was she being shanghaied? If help didn't arrive soon, she would end up on a ship far out to sea. She clutched the key in her pocket. Why did Dad drop it? It must be important, but how? Where was he?

Hairy Larry grabbed a lantern hanging from a nail in the wall. He struck a match on the wall and lit it. Light filled the tunnel, and dust motes floated in the air like snow.

"You'll get used to the dark, girls." Mr. Stickel rocked on his heels back and forth.

Sam clenched her fists. She wanted to wrap her fingers around his throat. She reached for Nicole's hand, and they followed Lawrence farther into the dark.

Nicole whispered. "What's the plan, Sam?"

She shrugged and began humming the tune to *Sesame Street*. Nicole's grip tightened as she picked up the tune and hummed along.

"They have a unique talent, Mr. Lawrence."

Sam quit humming, and Nicole sobbed. Mr. Lawrence held the lantern up to reveal a set of stairs and a sign, 1st Street and Stark. Mr. Stickel climbed to the top and turned.

"It might raise your price if you could only hum in harmony."

Mr. Stickel's laugh echoed down the tunnel.

****

The bare bulb cast shadows across Red's face as his frown deepened. Jim glared at the bricks, and Archie sat on a pile of dusty wood. The bricks had lost their glow. Jim put a hand on Red's shoulder.

Red slapped the bricks. "No, no, Jim, it went like this: *Our hands upon these bricks of clay*

Transport us through the

Something, something, etc. etc."

Jim shook his head. "It has to be exact. We're going to have to find a copy of the spell if one exists."

Archie stretched his arms over his head and yawned. Jim shot him a warning glance, but Red rushed him.

"Where are Mr. Stickel and the girls?" Red jabbed a finger at Archie. "They used the bricks to get away, and we presume they have gone to the Portland waterfront." Red took a step back and crossed his arms over his chest. "You are his assistant. You know the spell."

"I agree." Big Jim glared at Archie and stood beside Red. "I thought you were supposed to be helping us?"

"Umm, look here fellas. I didn't lose the key or the spell." Archie pulled his arms across his chest. He shrank as Jim towered over him.

He had lost the key, but why bring that up now? Aunt Eli had a soft spot for Archie, but he only got in the way. Jim clenched his fists. This was taking too long. Time was running out.

"There's a key?" Red glanced at Jim.

"He doesn't know what he's talking about." Jim shut his eyes and leaned against the wall.

"Focus on the bricks, Archie. We need to stop Stickel before he gets away with the money." Red glared at Archie.

Archie cleared his throat. "We must find Frederick. He might know the spell."

Big Jim pushed away from the wall. "Where is he?"

"Mr. Stickel has him in the tunnels as a hostage." Archie hung his head and stared at the floor.

"Why did you not tell us that before we came here?" Red shook his head.

Jim placed a hand on his shoulder. "We still need him, Red. Stickel will go to prison, and so will Archie, if he doesn't tell us everything."

"I am tired of these equivocations." Red grabbed Archie by the throat.

"No, Red." Big Jim shook Red by the shoulders. Archie's face had turned bright red.

Red released his hold, and Archie fell to the floor, backing away with a cough.

"Neither of you will get Stickel if you don't do as I say." Archie sat hunched over massaging his neck.

"Do not think that you are indispensable." Red turned and walked away.

Jim shrugged at Archie, then followed Red out of the room. Would Archie never learn?

Chapter 10

Misa To the Rescue

The tunnel disappeared into the dark. Occasional patches of light streamed down the stairs from the shops above. Sam clasped Nicole's hand as they shuffled behind Hairy Larry. Nicole flinched with each step as she hustled to stay in the light of his candle. The voices of shoppers filtered down to the tunnel. She wanted to call out, but the only one who would hear her over the bustle of shop noises was Mr. Lawrence. His long arms swung by his side. If she called out, he wouldn't hesitate to slap her or worse…

Nicole stumbled, and Sam steadied her balance. She pulled Nicole's arm over her shoulder.

"Thanks," Nicole mumbled. Her forehead dripped sweat. She wouldn't be able to keep up this pace much longer.

Sam tripped over a shoe, then stepped on a boot. They both stumbled. Sam hesitated, staring at all the shoes, but Mr. Lawrence glared.

"Watch your step, girls." Mr. Lawrence strode away with the lantern, and Sam pulled Nicole's arm tighter across her shoulder. They'd be in the dark if she didn't keep up with him, and Sam and the dark didn't mix well. Without the light, she'd be lost.

Sam stumbled over another shoe. The hair on her

neck prickled. These shoes and boots meant something. She couldn't focus, though, not if she was going to keep up with Mr. Lawrence.

"Was that a shoe?" Nicole's voice jarred Sam, but Mr. Lawrence ignored her.

Sam shrugged and avoided eye contact. "We probably won't like the answer."

He stopped and fit a key into a lock. The metallic clang grated on her nerves. Sam stood on her toes to peer around him, but he blocked her view. She had to get them out of this mess.

He pushed open a metal door made of bars, and it opened with a low moan. He grabbed her arm and pushed her through the door. Nicole fell in after her.

Bars. She spun around, but Hairy stood in the doorway. This was a cell.

"Now, give me a shoe."

"A shoe?" Nicole's tiny voice faded to silence.

Sam's mouth went dry. "You can't do this." She had difficulty getting air into her lungs. If he locks that door, we'll never get out. No one knows where we are.

Her fingers fumbled with the laces as she untied a shoe, and with a shaky hand, threw it in front of Hairy Larry. Nicole sat on the floor, dazed. Sam clenched her fists. He'd better not try anything, or she'd— What could she do to stop him? Nothing. Her shoulders slumped.

He held out his hand. "Come on girl." He stood tall, a glint in his eye. He had won. She wanted to wipe the grin off his face.

"Come here." Mr. Lawrence grabbed Nicole's shoe and pulled it from her foot. She sprawled onto her back, her head hitting the dirt floor.

"You're hurting her." Sam glared at Mr. Lawrence

as she dropped down beside Nicole. The door clanged as he slammed and locked it. He held the lantern high. Crude wooden bunk beds were built into the back wall, and an empty bucket, stinking of human waste, sat in the corner. A tremor ran from her head to her toes, and her stomach churned.

"The *Palisade Pearl* sails in the morning. I'm sure they have jobs for you during your voyage."

He stepped away from the cell, the lantern creating shadows that wavered across the floor and wall. shanghaied. She gasped. They were being shanghaied. She rushed to the door and shook it. It clattered but held firm. They were trapped.

"You can't do this." Nicole's shrill voice startled Sam.

Mr. Lawrence jangled the keys and whistled the tune to *Sesame Street*. He had been listening to them.

Sam shook the door again. "You'll never get away with this."

"Sleep well, girls. You have a big trip in your immediate futures." His lantern grew fainter. He turned a corner, and total darkness enveloped her.

"If we sail on the *Palisade Pearl*..." Nicole's voice shook.

"That's not going to happen." Sam clung to the bars to keep herself from falling.

"How are you going to stop it?" Nicole rustled to a stand. "He said the *Palisade Pearl* leaves in the morning."

"Let me think for a minute." Sam rubbed her chin.

"Well think fast," Nicole hissed. "Because we can't leave the bricks. How will we get home if we are at sea?"

Sam swung her arm through the air, searching for

Nicole, pulled her close once she found her. "I hear something."

"Wha—"

Sam put a finger to her lips and stared into the darkness. "It's coming from the other side of the wall." Sam clasped Nicole's arm. "Rats."

"Rats?" Nicole went still. "As in, darn it?"

"No, as in rodents."

Nicole tried to pull away, but Sam clung to her. The darkness covered her like a thick blanket. They must be far underground if light couldn't leak in from somewhere. Nicole leaned against her, the warmth calming.

"Listen." Soft footsteps approached, and Sam clung to Nicole.

Nicole's hand shook in Sam's. "This can't be happening. I want to go home."

"Quiet," a girl's voice said. "Do you want him to return?"

"Misa." Nicole hobbled toward the voice.

Sam pulled her back. "Henri's Misa?"

"Yes. It is I, Misa."

Sam shuffled along the wall with Nicole. "I can't see you."

"Hush," Misa whispered. "The tunnels have ears, and if you do not want to leave on the *Palisade Pearl*, you will do as I say. There is a board with a loose nail near the floor. Find it."

Sam let go of Nicole's hand, running her hands down the rough timber of the wall. The darkness made her dizzy. Misa didn't have a lantern or a candle. She must be able to see in the dark. Sam groped the wall, her panic rising like bile in her throat. "I don't feel any loose boards." She wanted to trust Misa. She had to or they'd sail with the morning tide.

"Shhh." Misa scratched a match on the wall and then light filled the area. Misa held out a candle. "Hurry."

The light oriented Sam, and she fumbled along the wall, her hands shaking. "Found it."

"Swing the board to the side, and you can squeeze through."

Nicole's warm hand rested on Sam's shoulder, giving her strength. She slid the board to the side. More light seeped in. Her dizziness evaporated, as she helped Nicole through the small space created by the board. Nicole clutched Misa in a bear hug, and the candlelight wavered.

"No," Sam gasped and scrambled through the opening.

Misa took Nicole's hand and squeezed it. She glanced from Nicole to Sam. "Follow me. We must hurry." Misa shaded the candle's flame, and it grew brighter.

The tightness in Sam's chest relaxed, but she raced after Misa, every pebble and lump on the floor bruising her bare foot. She gripped Nicole's hand as she hobbled.

The tunnel grew brighter. This wasn't the one that Hairy Larry had used. They must be closer to the surface. Dampness filled the air and stick figures were carved into the wood at every intersection. Misa followed the marks. She led them through a room filled with empty wooden boxes and furniture. Bees wax and turpentine mingled in the air.

Nicole jerked to stop, and Sam faltered. "My shirt."

"Shhh." Misa rushed to her and tore the sleeve of her sailor shirt from a nail.

"Oh." Nicole fell backward, but Sam caught her before she hit the ground.

"Shhh. Voices carry." Misa held out the candle. "We do not have much time."

"Quick. Keep up with her." Nicole stood and pushed Sam's hands away.

Sam rushed after Misa. They'd better get to where they were going soon before Nicole collapsed. Misa led them under a short doorway and through a stockroom room filled with lumpy burlap sacks. The scent of tea leaves and rosemary filled the air. Sam ducked under the low beam, waiting for Nicole to follow.

Light seeped down a stairwell, and Misa blew out the candle. She held up a hand. Sam pressed against the wall, her pulse pounding in her ears, her muscles tense. She couldn't run if she had to. Neither could Nicole. Misa held a finger to her lips and crouched. Sam pulled Nicole down beside her.

"I heard them. They went this way."

It was Mr. Lawrence, and he was close. He was talking to someone, hopefully not Mr. Stickel.

"We'll get 'em. They only have one shoe, right?"

It wasn't Mr. Stickel with Lawrence, but now the shoes made sense. The cruelty of taking a shoe hit her like an electric jolt. How could they—

"We can't lose them." The footsteps faded.

Sam shuddered. They were running away, so why did her legs still shake?

"This way," Misa whispered and rushed into the darkness.

****

Sam stumbled. She gritted her teeth as Nicole bumped into her again. Sam held Nicole's arm draped over her shoulder, and it took all her energy to keep up with Misa. She couldn't fall. If she did, she'd pull Nicole down with her, and they'd be caught. A crash and angry voices sparked her on, but Nicole tripped. How much longer could they keep this up? Light filtered through tiny cracks in the shops above them, revealing dust and cobwebs hanging from rough beams. She coughed to clear her throat.

"In here." Misa pulled them behind a half-wall.

Sam cowered next to a shaking Nicole as the stomp of booted feet approached. Misa held a finger to her lips and glanced over her shoulder. Once the men were passed, she tugged Sam's sleeve. Nicole grunted as Sam rushed after Misa into the darkness. How much longer would Nicole last? Perspiration beaded on Sam's forehead, and her upper lip. Why was it getting so warm and muggy? Sweat ran down her back.

"Are we close?" Nicole gasped. Her hand was sweaty in Sam's.

"Close to where?" Sam peered into the tunnel. Did Nicole know where they were going?

"Yes. We are near the laundry," Misa whispered.

Sam gritted her teeth. Nicole trusted Misa, so she had to, too. Misa was the key to their escape. The floor of the tunnel was slippery with mud, and Sam slipped.

Misa slowed her pace and turned to nod at Sam and Nicole. Was she checking to make sure they were still with her? Misa didn't explain but ducked through an arched door frame. Sam followed and blinked. They were in a room she did not recognize, but Nicole's arm relaxed. She knows where we are. This must be the laundry. Sheets hung like ghosts, white and frayed, on lines strung from one end of the room to the other.

"Is this Yabuki Laundry?" Sam wiped the sweat from her brow.

"Yes. Please keep your voice low." Misa led them deeper into the room away from sounds of splashing water and low voices speaking a language Sam didn't understand. "You will be safe by the folding tables. No one gets past Tetsu."

"Tetsu?" Sam stopped. "Who's Tetsu?"

Misa kept walking. "He is my oldest brother."

"What about Hairy Larry?" Nicole whispered.

"He only knows the main tunnels. They might make it this far, but my brother will distract them. He will never let them get this close."

"Shhh." Nicole pulled back a sheet and peered through hanging shirts and dresses. "I hear something."

There was a thump and the line near them hung with sheets began to sway. Nicole clamped one hand over her mouth and pointed at the line with her other, her eyes wide with fear.

The sheets billowed and swirled, and Sam couldn't move. Were her feet glued to the floor? Her stomach dropped. Someone was approaching, but who? She held her throat. Don't scream, don't scream.

An orange tabby cat with amber eyes appeared, its tail brushing through the sheets as it walked. It brushed up against Nicole's leg, and Nicole almost collapsed.

Sam slumped her hand falling from her throat. "You?"

"Is it yours?" Nicole reached to pet the cat. "It's so cute."

Misa scowled at the orange tabby cat. "No. This one showed up recently and won't stay away." She shook her head. "They are vile creatures."

Nicole pulled her hand back, and Misa stomped her foot. "Shoo?"

Orange fur and amber eyes—Aunt Eli's cat was so—

No. Sam shuddered. "Maybe he came back with me from Seattle."

Misa stooped to gaze at the cat. She frowned. "Many cats are ginger, but not all cats like water. This animal is unique." She lifted one of the cat's paws. It dripped water.

Aunt Eli's cat liked water, too. Sam felt the cat's neck for a collar and found none. The Duke never wore one either. The cat gazed at her and purred. "It must live down here, but it's so clean."

"It is well-fed, so it must have a home. Shoo, little *neko*. Someone misses you." Misa scooted the cat toward the arched doorway that led to the tunnels. They watched as its tail pulled through the sheets, just as it had when it arrived.

"That was weird." Nicole stared after the cat. She sank onto a chair by the wall.

"Now what?" Sam turned to Misa. "Where is Henri?"

"I do not know. I only know that she, too, is in danger." Misa wrung her hands.

"Henri is in danger?" Nicole stood. "Ow." She plopped down, rubbing her ankle.

"Mr. Stickel wants her on the *Palisade Pearl*. I was looking for her but found you instead."

"Henri? On the *Palisade Pearl*? We have to do something." Nicole's words were muffled by the clothes hanging in the damp heat of the washing room.

"Shhh." Misa placed her hand over Nicole's mouth.

"Do not worry. Tetsu is working with his friends to find her and the other girls. It is his mission to set the women free."

"But *The Palisade Pearl* sails in the morning." Nicole jumped from the chair and paced with a limp back and forth in the small space at the back of the laundry. "We have to help, somehow."

Sam scratched her head. What a mess. She'd really gotten Nicole into the doo-doo this time. Sam wanted to stop Dad from leaving, but somehow, she'd ended up in 1901. There must be a solution, but what was it? She had to work with Misa and Tetsu to save Henri. That was the only way.

Misa stared at Sam, then Nicole. Her black eyes seemed bottomless. "Do not worry, Mr. Stickel will not get Henri."

"How can you be certain? We have to hurry." Nicole pulled up her trouser leg, revealing a purple bruise.

"First, we must get Sam's disguise and wrap your ankle. Then we go." Misa bent down and ran her hand gently over the bruise. Nicole winced.

"I see Hairy Larry took one of your shoes." Misa disappeared behind the sheets.

"Where is she going?" Sam took a step to follow, but Nicole pulled her back, shaking her head. Her face was white. Sam nodded. Nicole trusted Misa, and she had to trust her, too.

Misa returned with a smelly bottle, a pile of clothes, and two pairs of boots. She placed the bottle on the table and held out the clothes. "You can change, while I tend to Nicole's ankle."

Misa grabbed a brown bottle. She poured the strong-smelling liquid onto a rag. Nicole winced as Misa began to rub the liniment into her ankle. Sam turned away, a knot in her stomach. Why had she touched the bricks? Too late to ask that now. She had to focus on saving Henri and getting back to the bricks and home. Could she do it?

Sam pulled on the brown wool pants and tightened a belt around the waist so they wouldn't fall. She scrunched up her nose as Misa rubbed more liniment onto Nicole's swollen ankle. Nicole grimaced but didn't make a peep. She just glared at Sam, who shrugged into a cotton button-down shirt that was white with thin blue stripes. At least she hadn't gotten a sailor suit like Nicole's.

Misa stood, hands on her hips. "Nicole must stay here, while Sam and I—"

"Oh no, you don't." Nicole crossed her arms over her chest. "I'm going with you."

Misa pressed Nicole's shoulders until she sat on the chair again. Nicole glared at Misa.

Misa took her hands and placed them on her lap. "You will only endanger yourself and us by slowing us down."

Misa was right, but Sam couldn't say that to Nicole, not now. She focused on lacing the scuffed old boots Misa had brought her then shoved her hands in her pockets.

"You have no choice. You must stay and rest."

Nicole scowled at Sam, then Misa. "I am not staying here alone."

"If we are to help Henri and rescue Mr. Stickel's other captives, Sam and I have to be able to run." Misa placed a hand on Nicole's shoulder. "You cannot run. I am so sorry."

Nicole's shoulders crumbled and tears streaked her cheeks. She was exhausted. They all were, but would Nicole try to follow them? Sam couldn't worry about that now. She pulled her hands out of her pockets and dashed through the sheets. Misa caught up to her at the doorway to the tunnel and tapped her shoulder.

"Here. You dropped this." Misa held out a key by the leather cord.

"Oh. Thanks." She stuffed the key in her pocket.

"Do not lose it. It will unlock answers for you soon."

Sam shivered. She needed answers, but what did the key unlock? She raced to catch up with Misa.

****

In the dim light, Jim could make out Lucky Star etched on the wooden crates and some of the barrels. He'd done it. Now he had to find Mr. Stickel before he transported back to Seattle.

"I did it." Red's eyes were as large as his smile.

Jim nodded and grinned. Red deserved a victory after the shock of going to the future.

Maybe Jim would explain how the bricks worked before he left, or maybe Elise would after they'd been married for a while. If he could get Red to marry Elise, it wouldn't matter. The names would reappear, and he could return to his family.

Red brushed off his trousers, then gave Big Jim a puzzled look. "So, where is he? We cannot have lost him after all that?"

"Mr. Stickel isn't going to make our job easy. You know that." Big Jim scanned the stockroom as he wiped the dust from his hands. "Archie, tell us where he is."

"He might have gone back to his bank." Archie sniffed and wiped his nose on his sleeve.

An overwhelming sense that time was slipping away washed over Jim. Sam's face flashed in his mind. Was he getting closer to solving the problem of the disappearing names? First, he had to stop Stickel.

Chapter 11

The Plot Thickens

Nicole sat on the stiff wooden chair in the laundry resting her leg on a crate. The towels and sheets strung on lines that crisscrossed the low-ceilinged room remained unmoving. Surely, Sam and Misa had found Henri by now. A clock chimed 1:30. They'd only been gone for fifteen minutes, but it seemed hours.

Footsteps approached, and she perched on the edge of the chair. They came closer, and she slipped off the chair and crouched under a table, putting a hand to her throat. The sheets waved as though pushed aside. Someone was coming for her. She pressed her back against the wall.

"She might be in the back."

It was Mr. Lawrence's deep voice mingled with the washer women's scolding voices. She scooted against the back wall.

"Ain't no one in here besides these laundry ladies, Larry, I'm tellin' ya."

He'd find her exposed, trapped, panicked, and he'd laugh that awful laugh. Nicole's hands shook and she clenched them into fists.

"Just let me check in the back, Buck."

Nicole's thighs ached from crouching. A breeze cooled her sweating face. She jumped as someone reached through a wall board and clasped her arm. She was caught. She opened her mouth to scream, but another hand clamped over her mouth.

"Silence," her captor whispered in her ear. "Misa sent me. Come quickly."

Misa. Nicole trusted Misa with her life. She had no choice but to trust this person. He pushed a board in the wall to the side. She scrambled to the wall. A strong hand helped her through the loose board and led her into a tunnel and around a corner then stopped. Light slanted in from an open door and seeped into the space where they stood.

"Who are you?"

"I'm Tetsu."

A boy a couple years older than she stood before her. He was six inches taller than she was. His distinct jawline and black eyes resembled Misa's—definitely her brother.

He motioned with his head to follow, and Nicole hobbled behind him. He came to a cabinet built into the wall. The door creaked as he opened it, and they crawled through an opening in the back.

It was like the wardrobe in *Narnia.* She raced after Tetsu down another tunnel at a crouch, the ceiling too low for him to stand. Nicole's ankle throbbed as she struggled to keep up. At least the bandage made it easier for her.

"Where are we going?" Nicole's voice echoed off the walls.

"Shh." Tetsu held a finger to his lips.

Her face burned. They must be far enough down the tunnel that Buck and Mr. Lawrence couldn't hear them, but still. She had to be cautious without being told.

"I am taking you someplace safe," the boy said, as he emerged out of the low tunnel and stood his full height. "No more questions. I will explain later."

He put his arm around her waist, and she didn't resist. His calm, quiet voice and slow movements reassured her. He'd helped many girls escape these tunnels, and now he was helping her. She relaxed against him, as he led her into the darkness.

****

Nicole let Tetsu drag her along. She hopped to protect her sprained ankle, a burden. She wanted to apologize, but he slowed before she could utter the words. She glanced up. A light glowed in the distance.

"Are we there yet?"

Tetsu ignored her, leading Nicole toward the light. His manner had become abrupt, business-like. She sagged against him as she took in the wooden crates stacked against one wall and bridles and a harness hanging from nails on another.

A lantern hung on the wall, and Nicole could make out the forms of two young women sitting in the semi-darkness. Their wrinkled dresses, dirt-smudged faces, and missing shoes told their story. A shiver ran down her spine.

"Who are they?" Nicole whispered.

"Women we have saved." Tetsu's voice cracked. He must be remembering his sister. "We will wait here for Misa."

"What will happen to them?"

"Once Misa comes, I will help these women get home. Misa said you were a girl."

Tetsu's gaze ran up and down Nicole. Her cheeks grew warm. Damn this sailor suit.

"I am a girl." Nicole bent and massaged her ankle. The bandage gave it support, but it still throbbed after their rush through the tunnels.

"You do not dress like any of the girls I know."

"Thank heavens. I know what happens to those girls." Nicole pointed at the women.

Tetsu clenched his fists. "Do not say that. It is not their fault."

Nicole glanced at the girls, then at the floor. She wiped her nose with her sleeve. She'd stuck her foot in it this time. A low mumbling came from behind the wall. These women lived in a man's world, and they didn't deserve this treatment. They were the lucky ones. They'd escaped, thanks to Tetsu. Nicole played with the tear in the sleeve. She'd wanted to save Henri, but her ankle made her useless.

"Why are they so quiet?"

"They are drugged and brought to a cell. If we do not release them. They would wake up on a ship far out to sea."

"Oh." She wanted to help Tetsu help them, but her stupid ankle made her a burden.

Tetsu walked to a corner where he sank into a squat. He picked up a stick and drew circles on the dirt floor. "Misa and I try to save as many as possible—since they took Akemi"

"Akemi. Misa told me."

"Yes. Our older sister." He sniffed and wiped his nose with the back of his hand. When he glanced at Nicole, his eyes glistened. "Can you imagine being torn from your family and never seeing them again?"

Nicole could imagine that because since she'd fallen into 1901 that reality made her heart race. "Yes." She wrung her hands. Misa must have told him part of her story, but did he know everything? She swallowed and forced back her tears.

Tetsu nodded. "Mr. Stickel's men drugged these women and brought them here, but we found them before they were put on the ship. They have a chance now."

Mr. Stickel. Nicole frowned. Of course, he was involved. "Mr. Lawrence works for him."

"He is a bad man. The authorities are trying to catch him, but he got away. He always seems to get away." Tetsu's voice faded to silence.

It always came back to Mr. Stickel, and Mr. Lawrence worked for him. Did Archie? And what about Big Jim and Red? All of them were connected to the bricks, but how?

Nicole sank to the floor with a sigh. "I hope Misa and Sam show up soon."

"I do, too." Tetsu stood and walked to the tunnel, gazing into the darkness.

Nicole lifted her sore ankle and placed it over her other leg to raise it. A million questions swirled through her mind. Tetsu's muscular form in the doorway gave her strength. He was saving women, and she wanted to help.

****

"They got away?" Frederick slumped in the chair he was tied to. "Do you have any idea what this means? You are complicating the spell, Archie. You know what happens when the spell becomes complicated?" Why had he ever listened to Cousin Charles?

"Yes, I do, as a matter of fact." Archie placed a hand on Frederick's shoulder. He didn't blink and his gaze never varied, as he held Frederick's gaze. "I'll find them. Just let me..."

"Quick. I can't spend another minute here. Untie me, so we can go back to the bank together."

"And what do you suppose we'll do once we get there?"

"You must continue to report to Mr. Stickel. Act like his plan can still work. I'll try to get home and convince Elise to help us." Frederick pulled against the ropes that held him. "We only have a matter of hours to break the spell."

****

Tetsu held a finger to his lips for silence. Footsteps approached down the tunnel, and they were coming fast. Nicole jumped to her feet as Sam, Misa, and Henri rushed into the room. Nicole's head spun as she sank to the floor.

Sam ran to her.

"I didn't know if—"

"We have to leave, now." Sam reached a hand to Nicole.

"Why? What's going on?" Nicole looked from Sam to Misa.

"Henri will lead you to safety. Your survival depends on getting out of these tunnels, at least until after the *Palisade Pearl* sails. Now go."

"But what about you?" Nicole couldn't leave now. She shook her head, but Sam wouldn't let her go.

Henri's hand trembled as she took the lantern from Misa. Tears glistened on her cheeks. Misa bowed and Tetsu crossed his arms over his chest. Nicole sighed and let Sam lead her into the tunnels.

****

Sam blinked. The darkness overwhelmed her making her dizzy as she tried to keep up with Henri.

Nicole hobbled on her sprained ankle, and Sam was torn between running to catch up and hanging back to stay with Nicole. At least her feet didn't slip anymore, but a chance meeting with Mr. Stickel or Mr. Lawrence kept her stomach tied in a knot.

"Agh." Nicole tripped, and Sam struggled to keep her from hitting the ground. They clung to each other.

"You must be quiet. Our voices carry in the tunnels." Henri frowned.

Nicole pointed to a thick-soled boot lying in the middle of the tunnel surrounded by boots and shoes some brown or black, some scuffed or shiny new. She saw men's wingtip shoes and loafers, but never a pair. "Oh no. More shoes."

Henri knelt before the boot. "The crimpers take one shoe or boot while their victim is passed out. Then they break bottles and spread the sharp pieces of glass outside of the cells to cut the bare feet of those who try to escape. Not very many people escape."

"That's what Lawrence did to us." Nicole put a hand to her throat. "Only without the broken glass."

"We must hurry." Henri led them around a corner.

Sam helped Nicole as they rushed to follow Henri down a tunnel. They branched to the left and then the right. Every tunnel seemed to have glittering shards of glass and single boots and shoes, and each one added up to men sent out on ships. Sam shuddered as glass crunched under her boots.

The darkness seemed endless, but soon they passed by a stockroom filled with shelves lined with jars of beans and peaches, another with small bottles of ointment and jars of cream.

Sam gasped in short bursts. They were running up a

slight hill, and water ran in rivulets along the right side of the tunnel. The dirt path became a boardwalk, and their footsteps rang out hollow and loud.

Henri jogged up the boardwalk until they came to a bridge and the tunnel came to a crossroad. Henri waited for them. She stood under a sign that read Sixth and Salmon. Henri's pale face in the candlelight glowed with perspiration.

"Tread carefully. The bridge is slick." Henri kept her voice low.

"Where are you taking us?" Nicole asked, her voice soft.

Henri pointed to the sign that Sam had noticed. "We are going to Goose Hallow. We will arrive at the Park Blocks, two blocks from here. It is far enough from the waterfront that we should be safe."

Nicole put a hand against the wall and lifted her sore ankle.

"What about Mr. Lawrence?" Sam's shrill voice startled her.

Henri held the candle and gazed into the tunnel. "I think we lost him. We must be quiet, though, or Mr. Lawrence will find us."

Sam braced herself to dash behind Henri, but she tiptoed across the wooden bridge without making a sound. She motioned for Nicole to follow. She did so in silence, even with her sprained ankle. Henri nodded at Sam. She stepped onto the bridge but caught her foot on the first board. She slipped.

"Ohhh." Her cry echoed off the walls as she stumbled. She was going to fall.

Everything happened in slow motion. Nicole's hand reached for her as she stumbled off the side of the bridge and splashed into the water. The shock of cold water made Sam gasp. Her heart pounded in her chest as she slid trying to stand, she slipped and fell again. This was how Mr. Lawrence would catch them.

Henri dropped the candle, and the darkness swallowed them. She groped in the dark and found Sam's hand. With a grunt, she pulled Sam back up onto the bridge. Sam leaned against Henri panting from the effort. Henri could have taken Nicole and kept going, but she stayed to save Sam.

"Thanks, Henri." Sam couldn't make out Henri's face, but she imagined her frowning. "I screwed up."

"I think I can guess what screwed up means, and you did," Henri whispered. "Hairy Larry and Buck have most likely heard that."

Sam froze. Nicole gasped and Henri stood helping Sam to her feet and off the bridge.

"Now we run." Henri and Nicole's footsteps moved into the dark.

Sam pushed herself to catch up with Nicole and Henri. She fought the dizziness, more afraid of being left behind.

Turning a corner, light seeped through the floorboards of a shop. They'd come to a storage room that smelled of sawdust. It was filled with stacks of rough-cut wood. Henri raced through a brick arch, and Sam huffed and puffed as the incline became even steeper, and Nicole lagged farther behind. They didn't have time to take a break, and if they did, Henri wouldn't stop to check if she were still behind her. They ran on, their short gasps echoing off the wood-framed ceiling and walls.

Sam squinted. It was a light, like a pinprick in the

distance. They rushed toward it, and it got larger. An opening to the outside? After the complete darkness of the tunnels, she wanted to weep for joy at the sight.

Henri paused and felt along the wall. Sam waited, the need to rush past her tempered by her curiosity. She trusted Henri, and if she stopped, there was a good reason.

"I hear voices ahead. Be still." Henri stepped off the boardwalk and into a side tunnel.

Nicole followed. Sam stood staring into the darkness. It would swallow her whole if she let it. She pressed her body against the tunnel wall for support and followed Nicole and Henri into the side tunnel.

Chapter 12

To Grandma's House We Go

Light from a lantern cast shadows on the main tunnel. Someone was up ahead and coming straight for them. Sam pressed her fist against her mouth as the footsteps of at least two people pounded on the boardwalk. Whomever it was didn't speak, but their exhalations echoed like a hiss as they came closer.

"Henri?" one of the voices called.

"Paul?" Henri stepped into the tunnel. "In here."

"Are you crazy?" Sam clutched her chest.

"It is okay. This is Paul and his little brother, Will. I told you about them."

Sam shrank against the wall. She reached for Nicole, but she caught only air. Paul hung the lantern on a nail and let it shine on them. Sam stepped back. There were two of them, but they were young, the older one her age. A seventeen-year-old and a fifteen-year-old against Stickel and Lawrence? They were screwed.

"Misa found you." Henri placed a hand on Paul's arm.

"Yes. We came as quickly as we could."

Sam put her hands on her hips. "How did you get from the waterfront all the way up here so fast?"

Henri frowned at Sam, her voice slow and deliberate, as though she were explaining to a small child. "They are messengers. They know all the shortcuts through town."

"I don't see bikes." Sam huffed. This was ridiculous. Sam's stomach tightened. They were so far away from the bricks now, they'd never get home. Sam kept her gaze on Paul.

"We ditched them at the Park Blocks' culvert. Smart thing to veer off the main tunnel. Hairy Larry was hard on your heels. He heard you before we did." Paul nodded at Henri.

Will took his hat off and brushed the hair off his forehead. "I had a feeling we'd find you in the Park Blocks."

"We had a little excitement at the bridge."

"We heard." Paul chuckled.

Sam wanted to crawl into the shadows. At least the darkness covered her burning cheeks.

"I too have fallen off that bridge." Paul nodded at her and grinned. "It is a slippery devil."

Sam gazed down at her muddy pants and hands. He was cute, and she was a mess. Perfect. "Yeah, I—" She paused. He was one hundred and thirty years older than she was. He wouldn't even be alive in her time. She cleared her throat, unable to speak.

Paul stepped back and the lantern illuminated Will. His eyes were a darker brown than Paul's with long black lashes and freckles across his nose. He blinked in the light. He hung back, letting his older brother take charge.

"We can't stay here." Paul held the lantern out so they could see their way.

"We'll take you to Grandma Meyer's. She's on 12th, but we should go now. Dinner will be on the board soon." Will brought up the rear as his brother led them toward the light.

"Board?" Sam shook her head.

"He doesn't want to interrupt their lunch," Henri said. "Do you think she'll help us?"

"Of course." Paul turned and led them away as Will hung back to help Henri and Nicole. Sam stuck close to the lantern. It kept her dizziness at bay.

"You must slow your pace," Will called. "Nicole has twisted her ankle and can't keep up."

Paul knelt by Nicole and shone the light on her ankle.

The light exposed dark purple bruising, and Sam winced. It was swollen, even wrapped.

"It is only two blocks to the bikes. She can make it that far. Then we ride." Paul lifted Nicole's arm over his shoulder.

Sunlight met them as they arrived at the culvert, and the warmth on her face melted the tension from her shoulders. A small stream flowed into the culvert, a cement pipe large enough for a man to stand up in. Sam gazed at Paul and Will as they helped Nicole.

Mr. Lawrence could follow. A shiver ran through her as she climbed the grassy embankment to a street lined with tall leafy trees after Paul and Will.

Black lampposts stood in a long row with ornate gas lamps hanging from them. A park lawn ran between two avenues with cement sidewalks for pedestrians to stroll along. Wooden benches sat on every block. Sunlight shining through the branches shaded the park creating a cool and inviting oasis. If she could only sink down on one of those benches and rest for a day or two.

Will whistled a warning, and Paul nodded. "Footsteps coming fast. Hurry." He rushed to two black bikes laying on the grass. "They cannot follow if they don't know which direction we go."

Sam kept glancing over her shoulder as she hopped on the seat of Will's bike. No Mr. Lawrence, yet. Will stood and pumped the pedals and they flew over the grass, across a sidewalk, and bumped onto a packed dirt road. Nicole sat on Paul's bike, and Henri perched on the handlebars as though she'd done it a hundred times. Paul stood on the pedals, pumping to gain speed.

Sam clung to Will's shirt as he pedaled up a slight incline. He grunted with the effort, but the bike picked up speed as it coasted down the other side. They flew into a neighborhood of large houses with manicured lawns. The road smelled like tar, and Will had to dodge potholes. Sam grabbed Will's waist as her hair whipped behind her. They caught up with Paul and rode side by side.

Will took his hands off the handlebars. "Yahoo."

Sam jumped, and the bike wobbled.

"Hey. Sit still."

"Hush," Henri said. "Do you want Hairy Larry to hear you?"

"Those two toughs will never find us in all these houses." Paul gripped the handlebars, smiling as he gazed down the hill over Henri's head. "Besides, the trees absorb sound. Whoo-hoo."

"Are you two crazy?" Nicole's curls ruffled in the wind as the bikes raced side by side.

The rush of the breeze across her face and the warm sun on her shoulders energized Sam. Her worries seemed to float away on the cool breeze. "Wahoo."

The bikes sped alongside streetcar tracks. A sign whizzed by, and she caught Jefferson Street. Paul leaned his bike to the right and turned onto 12th Street. It too was lined with trees, and the scent of roses filled the air as she gripped Will, trying not to tilt one way or the other. They coasted by large, stately houses, like something out of a fairy tale. The large front porches were shady and inviting, the windows reflecting the blue sky. Colorful flower-filled gardens and hedges framed it all.

"Where are you taking us?" Nicole's head bobbed from flowers to porches to hedges.

"Fancy-shmancy." Sam twisted her head to take in the yards and tall chimneys. "That house had five fireplaces."

"This neighborhood is pretty posh." Paul said with a grin.

"Posh?" Nicole shook her head.

"Rich," Henri explained, "like wealthy."

"You got that right. Grandma Meyer is posh, all right." Paul grabbed his hat before it flew from his head.

Sam gazed from Paul's sandy hair to his broad shoulders. His arm muscles rippled under his shirt as he held his bike steady with Henri balanced on the handlebars. Her stomach did a flip. Yep, he was cute.

"Is she your grandma?" Nicole asked.

"She's everyone's grandma." Will smiled at Nicole. "You'll love her."

Paul stood and pushed hard on his pedals. "She'll take you in for the price of a good story."

"A good wha—" Sam's stomach dropped as the bike picked up speed. With each pump, she was getting farther and farther from the bricks. She had to stop Will. Get him to take her back to the Lucky Star stockroom, but how, and could she trust Grandma Meyer? She sighed. At this rate, she'd never get home.

****

A tall, stern woman answered the door. Was this Grandma Meyer? But a grandma had white hair, right? This woman had dark hair pulled into a tight bun on top of her head. Whisps of curls escaped to frame her heart-shaped face and dimpled chin. Sam bit her bottom lip. This woman resembled someone, but whom?

Sam waited by the bikes with Henri and Nicole. Paul spoke in a hushed voice and gestured to the girls. Sam strained to make out his words, certain that he spoke about them. A tall hedge behind them acted as a protective shield, and she backed into it until the stiff leaves tickled her neck. The woman left Paul and Will on the porch. When she returned, a deeper frown furrowed her brow. Paul finally motioned for them to join him on the porch.

"This is Bertha, Grandma Meyer's cousin." He put a hand on Henri's shoulder. "This is Henri. I told you about her father." Henri lowered her head without losing eye contact with the older woman.

Will stepped aside so Nicole could hobble up to the door. "And this is Nicole and Sam. They have a story Grandma will find very interesting."

Sam hung back, taking in the shape of Bertha's face, her hair.

Bertha turned to focus on Sam, running her gaze from Sam's hair to her muddy boots. "Sam? Short for Samantha?" She nodded. "Boy's clothes. Good idea."

Sam tried to hold eye contact. She didn't want to offend this woman who could save them from Mr. Lawrence. She held out her hand, but Bertha ignored it.

"Grandma is in the library." Bertha's glare pierced right through Sam.

Paul settled his cap on his head as he backed down the stairs. "We'll be back with news of Mr. Stickel once we have it." Will followed him, and they hopped on their bikes, coasted down the drive, and disappeared around the hedge.

Bertha pointed. "Boots off."

Sam plopped on a step.

"A little help?" Nicole held on to the railing and eased herself onto the top step. Henri bustled over to help her.

Sam wiped her hands on her wool pants, waiting for Nicole and Henri. Her belly quivered, and she placed a hand on her stomach.

"Follow me." Bertha led the girls into a kitchen, through a dining room, and a parlor.

Sam checked for the key. It was still in her pocket. Will and Paul had left them here, so it had to be safe, right? Why was it the people she trusted left, like Misa or Tetsu or...Dad?

She chewed her cheek to stop her teeth from chattering. Bertha led them through a foyer, the marble floor shining. Stairs framed by a glistening oak banister rose to a landing that overlooked the front door. A crystal chandelier hung high on the ceiling. Bertha's heels clicked as she walked across the marble floor and led them into a room lined with shelves filled with books. The scent of lavender filled the room, and a white-haired woman with bright eyes and plump cheeks sat in an overstuffed chair a book on her lap.

So, this was Grandma Meyer. Bertha leaned to whisper in her ear. Windows opened to let in the fresh summer breeze, and light streamed in through side windows unobstructed by a porch. What a difference from the dark, muddy tunnels. Grandma placed the book on a table and smiled, her eyes swallowing them whole as she sat on the edge of her chair.

"Welcome girls." She sprang from her seat as if ejected by a spring.

Sam stepped back as Grandma Meyer took in their mud-stained pants and dirty hands and glanced at her couch. "Oh my."

"I'll fetch a sheet." Bertha turned and disappeared.

Grandma Meyer took Sam's hands and held them. "Welcome to my home. Bertha tells me that you have a story. I must hear it."

Sam melted at her warmth. Nicole wobbled and Grandma rushed to her side.

"You're hurt." Grandma bent to examine her ankle. She removed the bandage Misa had applied as Bertha returned with a large sheet and draped it over a sofa.

Grandma settled Nicole on the sofa. "We're going to need to soak this ankle in hot water, Bertha, dear, but first some refreshments." She glanced up at Nicole as Bertha bustled out of the library.

Sam sat next to Henri at the far end of the Sofa. Sunlight shone on the shelves of books that covered all four walls. She scanned the titles: *The Rise and Fall of the Roman Empire, The Encyclopedia of Botany, Casia et Tempus.* Glistening on the large oak table in the center of the room sat a porcelain figurine of a cat. Another cat?

She stared at her surroundings. She was living history, but how could she change it? The bricks might as well be a million miles away, as far away as Mom and Dad. Why couldn't Mr. Lawrence and Mr. Stickel be as far away? She shivered.

Bertha reappeared with a tray of cookies and pitcher

of iced tea.

The sweet aroma of the cookies filtered through the room. Sam took a glass and Bertha poured iced tea. She guzzled it down and sank back into the sofa and held the cool glass against her cheek. Henri and Nicole sat dropping cookie crumbs in their cloth napkins. Snickerdoodles, Dad's favorite. She couldn't eat. Rich maroon curtains framed the bright windows and dust mots floated through the beam of light streaming through the sheers. This was in 1901. This was real.

Grandma Meyer cleared her throat, and Sam jerked to attention.

"I understand that Mr. Stickel and Mr. Lawrence locked you in a cell, and that you were supposed to sail on the *Palisade Pearl*." Grandma Meyer stirred three sugar cubes into her iced tea, tinkling the sides with a silver spoon. "I cannot begin to tell you how angry I am at those two. But that is a story for another time."

A story for another time? Did she know Sam and Nicole were from the future? Did Bertha? Grandma Meyer's serene face gave away none of her thoughts. Her eyes were kind, and her short round figure and white bun pinned on the top of her head reminded Sam of a character out of a Beatrix Potter story, sweet but tough enough to bake someone into a pie if she had to.

"So, girls. Who wants to start?"

Henri cleared her throat and Sam nodded. She wouldn't have known where to begin.

"Mr. Lawrence caught Sam and Nicole and locked them in a cell..."

"In the tunnels?" Grandma Meyer set her spoon in her saucer with a clatter.

Nicole choked on her cookie, and Henri jerked her

head to stare at Grandma. Sam patted Nicole's back. She glanced at Grandma Meyer.

"Sorry, if I startled you, but I've been reading about such things." Grandma cleared her throat and patted a book that sat on the table beside her. "I'd never expect such a thing from Charles." She picked up the spoon and began to stir with a vengeance. "I detect a sadness in you, Henri. Your father has disappeared. Is that right?"

Henri nodded and focused on her hands in her lap.

Grandma had called him Charles. Did she mean Mr. Stickel?

"But you two," she said, looking first at Nicole then stopping on Sam. "There is a tension in you that I can't identify. It's like you don't belong here."

Sam's hand flew to her throat. Grandma knew. How did she know?

Grandma smiled at Sam. "Let's hear your part, and I promise not to interrupt."

Sam ran her fingers over the key in her pocket. It was warm. Maybe Grandma Meyer knew what it was for, but could she really trust this old woman? Sam had to take a chance, but how much should she say?

"Well...you see...it all began in Seattle in our time..."

"Your time? In the future?"

"Correct. It began with a school field trip where we heard a story about the bank that was never robbed, and the bank manager, Mr. Stickel..."

Grandma gasped. Why? She accepted the fact she was from the future, but she gasped at Stickel's name? Grandma held her napkin to her lips, her eyes scanning the books on the shelves. Sam clutched the key.

"So, Mr. Stickel went to your time?" Grandma

Meyer stood and walked to a shelf by the window. She ran her fingers over the spines of books, stopping on one and pulling it from the shelf.

Sam swallowed. The book cover was a deep purple velvet, the same color of the key's leather cord. That was a weird coincidence. "Yes. We saw Mr. Stickel in Seattle, and he wasn't alone." she stopped, the key becoming warmer in her hand.

"We saw Big Jim and Red. They were after us, but we don't know why." Nicole's words rushed from her like a flood.

Grandma nodded. "Did you—"

"Papa." Henri put a hand to her mouth. "You never told me."

Sam paused. "We wanted to, but—"

"Your father is part of this story, Henri." Grandma leaned over to pat Henri's hand. "But Sam and Nicole must finish their story. Then we may learn the part your father plays. Only then will we know how to solve this problem."

"Problem. That's an understatement," Nicole blurted.

Sam glared at Nicole, but Grandma nodded. She knew more than she let on. Should she mention the key? The bricks, the key, they were all connected somehow, and Grandma's reaction confirmed that.

"Why do Mr. Stickel and Mr. Lawrence want to hurt us?" Nicole's chin quivered as she spoke.

"I can't answer that until I hear all the details of how you arrived in Portland from Seattle." Grandma Meyer leaned forward, focused on Sam.

Should she mention that Big Jim looked suspiciously like her father? No. She had to stick to the basics. Henri placed a hand on Sam's, and Sam cleared her throat.

"We were on the Old Pioneers Underground Tour, in Seattle." If Grandma was going to help them, she needed to know everything.

"Underground?" Grandma Meyer's brows furrowed in concentration.

"You said no more interruptions." Sam rubbed her temple with her fingers. She just wanted to go home. She frowned at Grandma.

"I am sorry. I won't interrupt again. I promise." Grandma Meyer folded her hands in her lap. Bertha sat in stony silence beside Grandma in a cushioned chair with a carved wooden back. She hadn't moved or spoken since Sam began, but she was listening intently. What was her role in all of this?

Sam swallowed then began. "We were on the Underground Tour, and we heard the story of the bank that was never robbed and the murder with no bodies."

"Bank, murder?" Grandma put her fingers to her mouth. She sat back in her chair. "Sorry. I will be silent."

"Geez." Nicole set her glass on the table and glared at Grandma. "At this rate, school will be starting before Sam even gets to the part about the Roman Bricks."

Grandma gasped. "The Roman Bricks?" She glanced at Bertha, who had moved forward to the edge of her chair. "If the bricks are involved, this is more serious than I imagined. Seattle, Mr. Stickel, the underground, and the Roman Bricks?" She patted the book with the velvet cover on her lap.

She gripped the key. It grew warmer and warmer. Sam stared at the book. Was it—

Bertha sighed. "Where could that key be? I saw it in

here. I'm sure I did."

"It's not your fault, Bertha. Freddie probably took it along with the key to our vault." Grandma set the book on the table.

Sam pulled the key out of her pocket. The sun glinted off the black finish. "I have a key with the same purp-?"

Grandma gasped.

Chapter 13

The Library and the Key

Grandma stared at the key. "Where did you get that?"

"It fell from my father's pocket as he—"

Grandma held out her hand. "Why didn't you mention that before?" Grandma ran her fingers over the velvet cover of the book.

The sun was high in the sky as Grandma gave the book and the key to Bertha. Bertha fit the key into the lock and the lock clicked. The room was silent but for the ticking of the grandfather clock in the foyer. Bertha opened the book, and Grandma grinned as Bertha picked it up and carried it to a chair in the corner to read, oblivious to anyone.

Grandma turned to Sam. "She gets like that with a good book, and she's been wanting to open this one for a while. She must have time to read now, so maybe Sam can finish her story? Let me take you to a room upstairs."

What? Sam wanted to read the book too. "Bertha could read aloud."

"No, dear. She must read this on her own. It'll be faster."

Sam clenched her fists but followed Grandma out of the library. Henri helped Nicole to stand. Grandma and Bertha seemed to know about the bricks, which was good. And she didn't trust Mr. Stickel or Mr. Lawrence, also points in her favor.

The scent of lavender trailed after them up the stairs, and a wool carpet cushioned her stockinged feet, as she trudged behind Grandma. A skylight high in the ceiling let in enough light to make out crystal gaslights hanging on the wall. Grandma hesitated at the top of the stairs to wait for Nicole. They should be doing something. Bertha had unlocked the book, and she needed to read it, but...

She glanced below at the unusual floor where a star shape set in the marble graced the center. Aunt Eli's entry had a star just like that, but the elegance and beauty of Grandma Meyer's home outdid even Aunt Eli's.

Grandma led them into a room with windows all along the south wall. She walked to a closet door and opened it revealing a white tiled bathroom with a sink, a tub, and toilet. "You can freshen up if you like or lay down if you want." She motioned toward a twin bed against the wall and a couch across from the windows.

Sam nodded and sat on the edge of a bed. Grandma sank into a chair by the door, and Henri helped Nicole onto a bed. Sam told of the tour, and the stories they heard, the bricks, and landing in Portland. Nicole added to parts, and Henri corrected her twice, but she finally got to the end. Her eyes itched, and her throat was dry, but at least Grandma hadn't interrupted once this time.

Grandma sat back and shook her head. "You girls have had quite the adventure."

Bertha appeared at the door, and Grandma turned to her. "From what I've read so far, I think we need to—"

"Talk to Elise. I agree. Maybe she and Fre—"

"Yes. Freddie. We will need them both and the new information about the bri—"

Sam shivered. "The bricks started this whole problem." She glanced from Grandma to Bertha. They finished each other's sentences like they'd worked through problems like this before, but could she really trust them? Why had she given Grandma the key so quickly? It was too late now. "Who are Elise and Fre—"

"My grandchildren." Grandma clasped her hands in her lap. "Freddie. I have not heard from him in a week, and Elise has been avoiding me all day."

Bertha scoffed. "Elise is hiding something from you."

"You don't know that. It could be you she is hiding something from." Grandma glared at Bertha.

Nicole sat on the edge of the bed. "Wait. I don't get it. How are your grandchildren going to help us? Do they know Mr. Stickel?"

Bertha crossed her arms over her chest. "These girls are smart. Once Elise is here, they will be very helpful in finding a solution to this dilemma."

Nicole sank back on the bed and rubbed her ankle.

Grandma nodded. "Yes, but until then, they should rest. The work begins when Elise gets here. Oh, look at Nicole." Grandma glanced at Nicole rubbing her ankle. "You need aspirin and a cool compress for your ankle. They might be in the washroom cabinet."

"What about my fath—" Henri stood her fists clenched at her sides.

Grandma stood. "We can't do anything until I discuss what you've told me with my granddaughter. Now, rest. You will need your strength. I'll fetch the aspirin."

Need our strength? Sam opened her mouth, but Grandma's frown stopped her. She wasn't getting any more information from her. Sam rubbed her eyes. She was too tired to argue.

"Here, Nicole." Grandma handed her a glass and two pills. "I'll check back in half an hour." She walked to the door and pulled the door closed behind her.

A shiver ran up Sam's spine. Was this déjà vu? But it couldn't be. She hadn't even been born yet.

****

Henri paced the floor, and Nicole was using the washroom. Sam stared at her hands. It was only a matter of time before Henri asked about her father again. A knot had formed in Sam's stomach, and she had no answers.

"Please tell me again about my father." Henri's eyes sparkled with tears as she wrung her hands. "I cannot believe you saw him in your own time. How did he make the bricks work?"

Sam blinked. She sighed and sank onto the edge of a bed. Where did she begin? "He looked angry."

"Angry? Why?"

Sam shrugged. "He couldn't find Stickel, the bricks wouldn't work, and he wanted to come home."

"He did?" Henri leaned forward.

"Yes." Sam paused. What about her father? She wanted him home too. Sam smiled at Henri. "When they saw me, they tried to catch me."

"Father always sent word to me if he would be late or unable to come home, especially if it was for several days. At least he did until Big Jim showed up."

"Wait." A jolt ran through Sam's body. "Big Jim is new?"

"He arrived from the Headquarters in Washington D.C. about a week ago to help in father's investigation."

If Big Jim really came from Washington D.C., then

he was just another Secret Service agent. He couldn't be her father. Sam rubbed the back of her neck. "Why didn't you tell Grandma your dad knew Stickel?"

"Everything happened so quickly." Henri's eyes glazed over, and she was miles away as she sank back against her pillows. "Father was called in to do an audit. He told me large sums of money had disappeared from the Portland Trust and Savings Bank. When Big Jim arrived, they began an investigation on Mr. Stickel and that was the last time I saw him."

Sam taped her chin with her index finger. A week ago. That was when Mom found the lavender note, and Dad left. There must be a connection.

"I waited until the next day, but he did not return." Henri shrugged and shook her head. "The newspapers claimed that a bank in Seattle had been robbed. Mr. Stickel had disappeared, and police feared he had been murdered by two men with guns. However, no bodies were found."

"That's the same story our tour guide told us." Sam couldn't sit still another minute. She paced the length of the room. When would Bertha finish reading the book?

"That's when I went to Misa for help." Henri rubbed a hand over her cropped hair. "She cut off my ponytail, gave me these clothes, and introduced me to Paul and Will. They found me the job at the Lucky Star as their stockroom boy. Mr. Lawrence hired me, and over the week, I kept hearing Stickel's name. Turns out he's Lawrence's partner in the saloon."

Nicole limped out of the washroom. "What did you just say about Stickel? I was listening, but I missed that part."

Sam stopped pacing. "Stickel just happens to be Mr.

Lawrence's partner in the Lucky Star."

Nicole gasped. "His partner? If they are working together, it means they use the Lucky Star as a transport hub."

"OMG." Sam hugged Nicole. She could make the connections that no one else saw. It was like magic.

Nicole grinned at Sam. "That means that Mr. Stickel is very much alive, so no wonder no bodies were ever found."

"You mean my papa did not shoot him?" Henri sagged onto the edge of the bed. "Do you think Mr. Lawrence knew who I was and gave me that job to keep track of me?"

"That's exactly what I think, and I think your dad and the guy they call Big Jim are still hunting for him. I just wonder what his plan is?" Nicole reached into her pocket, pulled out a comb, and ran it through her tangled hair.

"Your father and Big Jim know about the Roman Bricks, but they don't seem to know how to use them. That's how Nicole and I got away from them." Sam rubbed her chin.

"But how *did* those bricks work?" Nicole hobbled into the room and plopped on a bed.

"I don't know, but I believe Grandma Meyer and her grandchildren know something, so we need them. Without their help, we won't be able to solve this mess." Henri sat in the bed, her eyes sparkling but not from tears this time.

"Archie seems to know how to use them." Nicole tapped her chin.

"Archie? That was your tour guide's name?" Henri asked. "Could he be Mr. Archibald Pisica, Mr. Stickel's new assistant? If it is, he does anything Mr. Stickel tells him to."

Sam frowned at Henri. "He's just Archie. Why?"

Henri bit her bottom lip, then spoke. "Archie disappeared when Mr. Stickel disappeared. I assumed he was fired because none of Mr. Stickel's assistants last very long."

"So, you think Archie works for Stickel?" Nicole stopped combing her hair and sat beside Henri.

"Well, he's also an informant for your dad." Sam brushed at her muddy pants and gave Nicole a shrug.

Nicole needed to get back to the present. What if her ankle was broken? They might be able to trust Grandma Meyer, but Sam didn't want to step near a 1901 hospital.

****

Mr. Stickel swiveled in his leather chair, an action his mother scolded him for every time he did it. What could she do now, though? Roll over in her grave? He grinned. Laughter trickled through the floor of the Lucky Star Saloon below him, and the familiar tug to join in tingled in his legs. Mother always said to hold himself above the rabble, but he wanted to join in. He would do just that once he was in Nome, Alaska. But first, he had to deal with Red and Big Jim.

Gazing out his office window, the wooden masts of ships being loaded with timber bobbed in the Willamette River. Dock workers called to one another on the docks as barges moved log booms and guided ships to their docks. It pulled him from the chair to the window. He should be long gone by now.

"Alaska, mmm." The gold rush made his pulse race, but first, those pesky girls must be on the *Palisade Pearl* and far out to sea. He paced the floor. Between the

Federal Agents and those time-traveling girls, how was he supposed to disappear without a trace? Not with everyone using the bricks.

He spun his chair to his desk and leaning forward, he ran his fingertips under the center drawer of his desk. With a click, he released the false bottom and let the board drop into his hands. He pulled the board out like a tray and sorted through the deed to his mining claim, the key to a safe deposit box in Seattle, and the one-way ticket to Alaska on the S.S. Portland. He returned it all to the board and clicked it back in place under his desk.

He shivered with pleasure. When would Lawrence get here? The *Palisade Pearl* had sailed, and now, he could disappear into the wilds of Alaska without a trace, shareholders be damned. It was his money, after all, and not even Mother's lawyers would find him.

His walking stick rested against his desk, and he leaned it against the window. He reached for a crystal decanter on his desk and poured golden liquid into a glass.

He raised it to the light and admired the amber glow. "To me and my future."

He drained the glass and cradled the heavy crystal tumbler. He would soon be rid of this office and all the shackles of this job. His shoulders shook, and he clutched his rotund belly as tears of laughter rolled down his cheeks.

Lawrence ran into the room. Finally. Stickel pulled out a handkerchief and dabbed his eyes. A frown wrinkled his brow. "I was just saying goodbye to this life once and for all."

"Goodbye?" Lawrence gazed out the window then back to Stickel.

He'll find out his role in this adventure soon enough, but by then I'll be gone.

"Mother never listened to me like you do, Lawrence. I told her I didn't want to be a banker. I wanted to be a cowboy. Do you know what she did?"

"No, sir."

"She laughed." Mr. Stickel sprang from his chair, and Mr. Lawrence took a step back.

"She said I would learn to run the bank, or I could lump it. I told her I'd rather captain one of her merchant vessels. 'Be a pirate is more like,' was her reply. Then I heard about Alaska, where real men go for adventure."

Lawrence stood at attention and nodded.

Stickel grinned. Lawrence was soon to be history, so he could speak the truth, at last. "I always despised this bank. Now she's dead, and thanks to Freddie and those bricks, I'm free."

Mr. Lawrence glanced around the room. "Is he still in the tunnels, sir?"

"Yes, and that is where he'll stay until I have made my last disappearing act. No one can stop me now." Stickel gazed at Lawrence and stuffed his handkerchief in his pants pocket. "Now tell me that those horrid girls are on the *Palisade Pearl*. Won't they be surprised when they wake up in New Brunswick?"

Why was Lawrence gazing out the window? Stickel glanced over his shoulder.

Lawrence shuffled from foot to foot. "That's what I came to tell you, sir."

"Stand still man." Stickel frowned.

Lawrence threw his shoulders back and grimaced. "The *Palisade Pearl* sailed without th—"

"They escaped?" He grabbed his cane and strode

around the desk. He raised his arm, and Lawrence stood speechless. A crack filled the air, and Lawrence dropped to a knee.

"You idiot. What do I pay you for? You call yourself a manager? What have you managed? You've managed to destroy all my plans; that's what you've managed. So where are they now?"

"D-d-disappeared." Lawrence cleared his throat. "But, sir, there's more."

"More? This just gets better and better, you-you-you, fly in the soup." Mr. Stickel clenched his fists.

"I…" Mr. Lawrence paused.

"Mr. Stickel." Archie rushed into the office. His cowering was so annoying. He'd fire this useless scoundrel if he weren't leaving. Archie brushed dust off his vest, his amber eyes unblinking. Stickel ground his teeth.

"I have news, sir." Archie gave a slight bow and nodded in Mr. Lawrence's direction.

Why does he never blink? Mr. Stickel braced himself. He had no idea what Archie's news might be.

"Red and Big Jim are back in Portland." Archie stared Mr. Stickel straight in the eye.

What insolence. "Back? What do you mean back? Did they figure out how to use the bricks?" Why was the room getting so hot? Stickel pulled a handkerchief from his pocket and wiped his brow. "You cannot mean it because that would ruin all my beautiful Alaska plans." Stickel lowered his voice. "And why did *you* leave Seattle? That was not the plan."

Archie took a step back. "Umm." Archie tensed. He angled toward the door and shuffled his feet, glancing from Stickel to Lawrence whose eyes never left the floor.

"Is Freddie still where you left him?"

Archie nodded. Mr. Stickel swung his walking stick up and holding it like a bat, swung at him. Archie dropped like a stone.

Mr. Lawrence cleared his throat.

"What." Mr. Stickel wiped the blood off his walking stick with his handkerchief.

"I was hoping to get him to reveal where Freddie was." Mr. Lawrence pulled thumb screws from his pocket. The vice-like objects fell to the floor

Mr. Stickel turned to the window. "Apparently, I'll find Freddie myself, and when I do, I won't need those antique torture devices." Mr. Stickel slipped his hand into his pocket. The cool metal of a gun lent him strength. Show no fear. That was Mother's motto. "Your usefulness to me has expired, as well." Mr. Stickel turned and in one motion, pointed the gun and pulled the trigger. The revolver clicked. He pulled the trigger again. Click.

Had he forgotten to put the bullets in? Again?

Lawrence spun and ran out the door.

"Damn you to hell." Mr. Stickel stomped his foot. "Fine. Good riddance, Lawrence."

Mr. Stickel opened the bottom drawer in his desk. He grabbed bullets and put one in each cylinder then snapped the chamber closed and slipped the gun into his pocket. He ran his fingers under the center drawer, clicked the latch, and pulled the board out like a tray, setting it on the desktop.

He tucked the key, the papers, and the ticket into the breast pocket of his jacket, then stood. "Mr. Charles Mortimer Stickel, it is up to you to get this plan back on track. Now."

He adjusted his lapels and strode out of his office humming the tune to *Sesame Street*.

Chapter 14

The Book

Misa rummaged through the discarded clothes box under the folding table as Red and Big Jim washed up at the sink. She pulled out a suit jacket with broad shoulders and sleeves long enough to fit Red's frame. She set aside a pair of dungarees. They would not be suitable for approaching Stickel, the president of the Portland Savings and Loan then stopping him from stealing money from the hardworking local people.

The only way to stop that villain was to catch him and throw him in jail. Misa pulled out a second suit jacket for Big Jim. Plus, catching him would save the lives of so many men and women, like Akemi. Misa bowed her head. They had to catch Stickel. It was too late for her sister, and possibly Freddie, but it would save other unfortunate souls.

She wiped away her tears. This was not the time to cry. She pulled out two white dress shirts from the box. Red and Big Jim would make sure no one else had to go through the pain she and her family had gone through.

"Were you able to find Frederick Meyer?" Misa focused on the shirt she held in her hands, afraid of the answer she'd hear.

Big Jim's large hand on her shoulder startled her. Had he guessed her feelings for Freddie? He shook his head. She tucked those feelings away again. They didn't matter, not if he was stuck in the future, or—

"We have to find him if we are going to stop Mr. Stickel." Big Jim smiled, and she gave a slight bow.

"Quickly, James. Time is running out." Red reached for the walking cane with the brass goose head handle leaning against the wall. He spun it before him and tapped it on the floor.

"Nice touch," Jim said.

"Here. Don't forget these." Misa brushed lint off a bowler and handed it to Big Jim. She nodded approval. The pot-bellied Mr. Ladd would never recognize his jacket on Big Jim.

"Thank you." Red donned the Fedora and turned to Big Jim. "Shall we?"

"We shall." Big Jim tipped his cap at Misa.

Towels bobbed on the lines as Big Jim and Red made their way through the laundry to the tunnels. She rubbed the back of her neck as she picked up the "Wanted" poster and gazed at it. She gave a crisp nod. No one would mistake the clean-shaven, well-dressed men who had just left for the criminals in these photos.

"May luck be with you," she whispered. "Your daughters' lives depend on your success."

****

Grandma's and Bertha's voices filtered out of the library and up the stairs. Sam could make out occasional words—bricks—tunnels—bank. She tiptoed out of the room and stood on the landing above the entry, between Nicole and Henri.

A key jangled in the front door, and they scrambled into the hallway leading to the bedrooms. Henri ran back to the room but stopped. A young woman walked in, and

Grandma and Bertha rushed to greet her. Sam leaned forward. This must be Elise. She needed to speak to her, but Nicole grabbed her arm, shaking her head. Sam frowned but sank down beside her.

Nicole whispered in her ear. "They might say something to each other that they wouldn't say to us."

"Tell us everything, Elise." Grandma Meyer's voice was brisk as she led Elise into the library. "Can we save them?"

Save them? Grandma's words stung like a slap. Had she known about Sam and Nicole before they arrived? Sam lifted a hand to her cheek.

Elise glared at Grandma. "You mean the girls you're hiding upstairs that the whole neighborhood knows about? The spell runs out at midnight, so it is unlikely."

Sam tensed. A time limit? They never would have said this to Sam or Henri. The front door stood open, and a breeze filled with the aroma of lavender feathered across Sam's cheek.

"What about Freddie? We received the letter from the bank five days ago and nothing since. Cousin Charles still has him and who knows—"

"I know, dear." Grandma's voice softened.

"Cousin Charles?" Sam met Henri's gaze.

"That must be Mr. Stickel." Henri frowned at her.

Sam stood. "We have to get in there."

"No." Henri put a hand on Sam's arm. "We need to listen. Nicole is right. They won't speak freely with us in the room."

Sam nodded. Well, she could at least get closer. She slid down a step. Nicole slipped in beside her and Henri followed, her focus never leaving the library door.

"Charles's recklessness knows no bounds. No one

can recover the bank funds but us, and he wants that money for his Alaskan adventure." Elise paused, a hand to her breast. "Freddie is in immediate danger, so rescuing him must come first."

"You are right." Grandma Meyer sighed. "But this all could have been avoided if Freddie had come to me the first time Charles approached him about those gosh-darned bricks."

"Delores—"

Grandma cut Bertha off. "If Bertha and I were there, we could have stopped that madman."

Was Grandma blaming Elise? Sam nudged Nicole who shook her head. Eavesdropping raised more questions than it answered. She scooted down another step.

"Freddie is involved, too?" Nicole mouthed as she slid down next to Sam.

Sam shrugged and wrapped her arms around her torso. She needed answers, not more problems, but Freddie was now part of the problem.

"The biggest mistake of my life was listening to Freddie. He didn't want me to confide in you. He trusted Charles in a hero-worship manner. What a mistake."

Sam's arm tightened around Nicole. They scooted down two steps.

"If Grandma and Elise are related to Stickel, whose side were they on? I told her my whole story, but she's told us nothing." A knot tightened in Sam's stomach.

The springs in Grandma's chair squeaked, and Elise paced in front of the door. Sam pulled her feet up in case Elise glanced her way.

"He is insane." Grandma's voice held a tinge of anger. "I'm just glad Harriet isn't alive because Charles' behavior would kill her if she wasn't already dead."

"He won't be able to use the bricks again, will he? Not without me and Freddie." Elise leaned against the door frame, clutching her hands to her chest.

"He already has. Besides, he has broken the first rule of the bricks. Never use them for greed." Grandma's chair squeaked as she adjusted in the chair. "He has no idea the damage he's caused."

"The bricks have rules?" Nicole whispered. Sam put a finger to her lips, and they all scooted down a step.

"Start at the beginning," Grandma said. "How did you and Frederick activate the bricks?"

"Ugh." Sam slumped back on the stair. Would the storytelling never end? Nicole raised a finger to her lips and frowned.

"Frederick took the position at the bank, and Charles immediately pretended to take him under his wing, as a favor to you. Soon, Freddie would do anything for him." Elise paced by the door to the parlor going in and out of view. "He needed a father figure, you know. Freddie invited me to lunch with him and Charles, and I went."

"If I'd known he was losing his mind, I'd never have encouraged Frederick to take that position." Grandma Meyer's heels clicked on the wood floor. "I just don't understand how Mr. Stickel knew Freddie held the power?"

"They both do," Bertha said. "They are twins remember. It takes them both to initiate the bricks."

"I know but—" Elise sobbed.

Grandma was patting Elise by the sound of it. "How is he able to use the bricks without either of you? Is that why he is keeping Freddie?"

Sam let out a shaky sigh. And to think, all she

wanted to do this morning was destroy the lavender note and get her father back. Simple. But nothing about those bricks was simple, and she still didn't understand how she got them to work.

"Now that they are active, he must be reciting the spell." Elise began to weep. "All I know is we don't have much time to stop him before the spell breaks down, and Freddie will be lost forever. If the bricks stop working, those poor girls could be stuck here." Elise wrung her hands.

"Stuck in 1901?" Sam reached for Nicole's hand and stood. Henri's chin was trembling. Time was running out, she might be stuck here, and Henri's father might never return."

"You are right, dear." Grandma blew her nose. "We don't want that to happen—again."

"Again?" Sam clapped a hand over her mouth.

"Bertha." Nicole nodded.

"Bertha used the bricks?" Henri frowned at Nicole.

Sam pulled Nicole behind her as she stepped into the library. Nicole clung to her for support. Henri followed.

"That means the story about the girl who disappeared is true." Sam clung to Nicole's.

"What are you gir—" Grandma popped off the couch, and Sam took a step back.

"You don't think that Charles has figured out they are here in the house, do you?" Elise glared at the girls.

Sam shivered. "If Mr. Stickel finds us, we'll never get home."

"If Stickel suspects they are here, he will come for them." Bertha gazed from Elise to Grandma, her back ramrod straight. "This book does have answers. We only have until midnight to return them before the bricks lose their magic."

****

Why did she give Grandma her key, and why didn't Grandma start giving her the information she needed, and why was this house so warm? Sam wiped her brow. Elise stared at her like she'd seen a ghost. Grandma and Bertha stood silent as they approached. Grandma had expected this interruption.

Sam glared at Grandma. "We need to know everything, so we can help formulate a plan."

Nicole nudged her and shook her head.

Grandma closed her eyes and gave Bertha a nod. "She's right."

"I've been reading about the creation of the bricks." Bertha patted the book with the purple velvet cover on the table beside her chair.

Bertha nodded and glanced at Elise. "So, this is what I've learned so far. You come from a long line of mages."

"Stop." Elise lifted her hand. "These girls should not be given our family secrets."

"You are wrong. They must know everything, Elise. Their lives depend on this knowledge." Grandma sank into her chair.

Sam walked to the sofa, sinking into the cushions. Nicole plopped down beside her.

"Tell us," Nicole said as Henri scurried to join her.

"First Freddie and now these girls, those bricks are pure evil." Elise hung her head.

"Buck up, dear." Bertha placed a hand on Elise's shoulder. "Those bricks are connected to your family through blood, sweat, and tears. I will start at the beginning in order to help us understand this present situation."

"Fine." Elise stood by the fireplace scrutinizing her cuticles.

Bertha folded her hands in her lap. "I wasn't certain until now, but it seems you and Freddie have inherited the family gift. Your father di—"

"You call this a gift? It is not." Elise paced the library floor.

"No more outbursts." Grandma glared at Elise. "Bertha has the floor."

Sam folded her arms over her chest. Elise stood by the fireplace her arms folded across her chest, and Grandma sat at attention. She motioned with her hand for Bertha to continue. It was like some secret meeting of the Order of the Bricks.

Bertha cleared her throat. "As I was saying, the Meyer family originated from a long line of Mages and Druids from the Alba-Iulia region of Romania. They were farmers, but the Romans ruled that area and they needed free labor from the locals to make bricks for their roads and other structures."

"Hmph." Elise scoffed.

Grandma sighed and threw her hands in the air. "Elise, what is wrong with you? You grew up with those bricks. You loved the double stamp and the cat's paw prints. You'd trace them with your finger. Remember? They aren't evil. The people who misuse them are evil."

"You warned me about the bricks. I wish I'd listened." Elise sank into a chair. "If you think hearing Bertha retell this story will help us solve this problem, so be it."

Grandma nodded for Bertha to continue.

"In the year 377 BC, one of your ancestors, Guillem the Wise, lived with his family on a farm in

Transylvania."

"Did you say 377 BC? Transylvania?" Nicole frowned. "That's like before Dracula, right?"

Sam nudged her.

Bertha ignored the interruption. "Guillem was a druid and spiritual leader in his village. When the Romans came to conscript men to manufacture bricks for Roman roads and buildings, the fields were ready to harvest. He knew if the village didn't bring the crops in, they would starve over the winter. He refused to work, and his neighbors stood with him.

"The Romans knew that without Guillen, the others would fall in line and make the bricks, so they sentenced him to death. They dragged him to the brickyard, his friends and family following, begging for his life. His wife, Myra, his sons, and friends were forced to watch in horror as the life was whipped out of him."

"Why must these stories always end in death?" Elise frowned at Sam and Nicole. "The answer might be somewhere in these stories, but how will hearing this help them get home?"

"I will not ask you again, child." Grandma pounded a fist on the table beside her. Elise jumped in her chair and sat back clamping her mouth shut.

Sam glanced at Elise. Why didn't she want Bertha to tell the story? Was it that big a secret?

Bertha smoothed the front of her dress with her hands and began again. "That evening, under the light of a full moon, Myra, Guillem's wife, and his three sons returned to the brickyard. They gathered the clay from the factory yard that had been saturated with Guillem's blood and made two flats of what are now known as the Alba Iulia bricks or Roman bricks.

"During that time, the Roman Legions stamped each brick with the legion number of the area and a symbol of the region, which in this case was an eagle. Myra and her sons marked the bricks they made with a double stamp so that they could identify them. The double stamp turned the Roman Legion numeral III into a triple X. That night as the bricks dried under the full moon, Guillem's grieving cat walked across them, leaving paw prints that embossed their own magic into the clay." Bertha paused.

"Wow. That's love." Nicole shook her head, her eyes filled with tears.

"We must focus on the bricks, not the cat." Grandma gave Bertha a curt nod.

"The cat is significant, but as you wish." Bertha sighed. "Myra and her sons stole those bricks after they'd been fired in the kiln, and for years the wife would hold the bricks and cry over them, grieving for her beloved husband. The salt of her tears became one with the chemical makeup of the bricks just as her sweat, his blood, and the cat's love in the paw prints did. These elements instilled the bricks with their power."

Grandma gazed from Sam to Elise, and Sam's stomach flip-flopped. "Oh. I see it now. Love is the most important element." Grandma stood and walked to Elise. "I see it in your dark hair, your brown eyes, the shape of your chin."

"What do you see?" Elise sat on the edge of her seat, her face pale.

The world spun, and Sam couldn't get her bearings. Was Grandma describing her or Elise? She clutched the edge of the couch cushion.

"Sam, where are your people from?" Grandma

stirred sugar into her tea.

Sam's throat constricted. She coughed and cleared her throat. "The Greats?"

"Greats?" Grandma asked.

"Do you mean my ancestors? The Greats are all my great-great-great-grandparents. Maybe Romania? Aunt Eli has a Bible from there, so…"

"Romania. Of course. And where did you get this key?" Grandma held the key up by the cord.

Sam's mind raced. She hated tests, and this sure seemed like one. "My dad dropped it. I think he got it from Aunt Eli who has the Bible."

Elise gasped. "Bible?" She raised a hand and clutched it to her chest.

"This Bible?" Grandma pulled a book from the shelf.

It had a green leather cover with gold letters spelling foreign words. It was *the* Bible.

"What? How?" Sam's heart pounded and spots swirled before her. She clenched her teeth and counted to ten. Dad, He'd be so proud.

"Sam is connected." Bertha rose and walked to Sam.

The hair on her arms rose. "Connected? Is that why the bricks worked for me, brought me here?" Sam paused. "Hey, are we related or something?"

Grandma nodded. "If only people who share Guillem's blood can use the bricks, we must be. But it was my father who had the gift, and then it passed to my son, and now Freddie and Elise, but not my own. That's why I couldn't help Bertha." She glanced at her friend. "Now you must have the gift, Sam, so you will need to understand how to use them properly so we can get you home."

Bertha wobbled and reached for the fireplace. Sam couldn't move as Grandma rose and placed a hand over Bertha's. It trembled.

"Bertha? Are you okay?"

"Your Aunt Eli…" Bertha bent like an old woman, leaning against the bricks of the fireplace, her face as pale as stone. "It's just that I miss them so much."

Sam stared at her. Had she been stuck here all these years? She's an old woman now. Sam bit her lip.

"I know, dear. Has it been forty-nine years?" Grandma patted Bertha's hand, but Bertha stood unmoving.

"Forty-nine years, three months, and thirteen days, and what time is it?" Bertha pulled a handkerchief from a pocket in her dress and dabbed at her nose.

"So, you do keep track. I thought so." Grandma held Bertha's hand. "You must not forget that I lost people too, a son who was more precious than my own life, and his beautiful wife. Bless their souls. She believed in him when even his own father doubted and feared his gift."

"Quit talking of it as his *gift*." Elise sprang from her chair. "It was not a gift if it killed him."

"They didn't die." Grandma wrung her hands. "They just didn't come back to this time."

"What?" Elise spun around to face Grandma. Her eyes were round, and her mouth poised for speech, but no words came out.

"A gift can sometimes be a double-edged sword." Bertha lowered her gaze.

"I don't understand." Elise frowned.

Bertha patted the book. "Each generation a family member chosen by the ancient cat guards the bricks." Bertha glared at Grandma. "And the cat is as important as the bricks."

"We do not know that for certain." Grandma glowered at Bertha from her chair.

The room spun, and Sam clung to the arm of the couch. Cat? Ginger cat?

"Elise, the gift can also bring great joy. The sooner you realize that the better." Grandma kept a steady gaze on Elise. "And it is the only way we can help Sam and Nicole."

A chill ran down Sam's spine. Grandma was talking in riddles and code. Elise wrung her hands and shook her head. She jumped from her seat and rushed out of room. The front door slammed, and the echo reverberated through the house. Sam clutched Nicole's hand, the tension in the air thick and cloying.

Bertha moved to stand behind Grandma's chair like a sentinel holding the purple book under one arm.

Grandma tapped her chin with a finger. "The game is afoot, Bertha."

Chapter 15

A New Mission

Mr. Stickel smoothed his thin hair with his hand. He stood in the storeroom under the Lucky Star and scanned the wall looking for the bricks, but they no longer glowed. He recited the spell; nothing happened. He stomped his foot.

"Those brats. I missed my steamer, and for that, they shall pay." He frowned as he gazed into the darkness of the tunnel. The door upstairs opened. Someone was coming. They had a light step. It must be the new barmaid, Sally, coming for bottles of rum or whiskey. He hid in the shadows until he saw her face come into view, then he reached out and grabbed her wrist. She screamed.

"I was hoping I would find you, Sally," Mr. Stickel said and chuckled. He caught his reflection in an old mirror. His suit was speckled with dust, and his hair stood on end.

"Mr. Stickel?" Sally tried to pull her hand away. "They said you'd been murdered." She was white as a ghost.

Good. He liked it when they were afraid of him. She yanked her arm again. She was strong, but Stickel was stronger. She wouldn't get away.

She stopped pulling and stared at him. "I knew something was up. Mr. Lawrence has been a tyrant for the last two days, ever since you disappeared."

"Lawrence? Well, he's a pussycat compared to me." Mr. Stickel laughed. "I owe someone some cargo, and you are going to help me settle up."

"What? Settle up?" Sally braced her feet. "You can't do this."

"Oh, but I can." He gripped her arm and tugged.

She glared at him and hissed. "You'll never get away with this. My sis and that Henri-kid will—"

"Will what? Rescue you? Hardly, my dear." Mr. Stickel dragged her into the tunnel. "Don't worry about your sister or Henri. You are going to help me find them before you leave."

"No!" She twisted and dug in her heels as he hauled her into the gloom.

****

The sound of tugboat whistles and horns filled the air. Longshoremen shouted to one another as they loaded and unloaded cargo onto ships. The Portland waterfront was magnificent. Jim filled his lungs with fresh river air. He was living history, but he wouldn't have time to enjoy it.

"How many of these men will be shanghaied, do you think?" Jim scanned the length of the waterfront at all the men scurrying like ants to load and unload boxes and crates from several ships.

"A lot less of them, once we capture Stickel." Red's gaze took in the waterfront scene as gulls shrieked overhead. "Where to?"

"I have an idea." Jim cleared his throat. "We should head to the Park Blocks, where Stickel lives. We might catch sight of him or the girls." It was a longshot, but Elise Meyer also lived there, and if they ran across her, and somehow Red could meet her, maybe he could check an item off his stop-the-names-from-disappearing list.

"If not, we'll head back here to the Lucky Star and pay a visit to Lawrence. I'll bet he knows where the girls are. I'm ready to get rough if we have to." Jim glanced at Red. Had he taken the bait? How else could he get him to meet the future Mrs. McCluskey?

"Our original mission was to stop Mr. Stickel before he escaped with the money. It did not involve any girls or Mr. Lawrence." Red cocked his eyebrow at Jim.

Red had impressive focus. He'd followed Stickel to the future and hadn't even realized he'd left 1901. He was like a bulldog after a villain stealing from his own bank. He should get a medal, but how would they write the report and not sound insane?

"We have a *new* mission." Jim let his words sink in.

Red frowned. "But we are so close to catching Stickel. What do you mean?"

Jim nodded. "I know, but we have minors involved now. We need to find the girls and get them safely home before we go after Stickel."

"True. We are honor bound to protect the innocent, and if we get the opportunity to stop a crimper, even better." Red scanned the docks.

Jim grinned. He had nothing but admiration for his great, great-grandfather. An overwhelming desire to tell him the truth hit him. It would make this so much easier, but maybe it wouldn't. If Red thought he was crazy, his mission would fail, and Sam…

Jim shook his head. "The girls come first then."

"Agreed. Stickel is unpredictable, which makes him dangerous." Red rubbed his chin. "When he is finally behind bars, I am applying for a desk job in Portland.

This case could be my last in the field." Red's eye twitched. It was the only sign of his fear.

"We better hurry." Jim rushed up the hill to the Park Blocks. Red still had to meet Elise and fall in love before midnight, or he'd be stuck in 1901 with Sam.

****

The sun shone high in the sky and bird song filtered from the trees as Red and Jim sauntered down the Park Blocks. Mothers pushed wicker baby carriages, and men strolled with newspapers rolled under their arms. This could be any day in Seattle, except for the lack of cars and the wool suits in summertime. Jim wiped his brow. He had to keep an eye out for Sam and Mr. Stickel.

"Let's find a bench in the shade and talk through our plan one more time." Red pointed across the street. "There's one."

Red ran in front of a horse-drawn carriage. Jim waited for the driver to rattle by without a glance at Red. Jim glared after the carriage. Drivers were the same in any time period. Jerks.

He opened his mouth to complain about the carriage as a young woman rushed toward them. Could it be her? Her skirt swayed with each step, and her lace collar flounced. Pale blue forget-me-nots were embroidered on the hem, just as they were in the picture Aunt Eli had shown him. His mouth went dry. It had to be her. This was Elise. He had found her, but how did he get Red to notice her?

She was headed for the same bench Red had pointed to, and Jim took a step back. She was dabbing at her eyes as she ran into Red. Red frowned but stopped, and his face went blank. Jim scratched his head. Was the universe on his side now?

"Oh, excuse me miss." Red reached out to steady the young woman who stumbled. She paused in confusion, looking from the bench to Red.

"No, pardon me. I was not watching where I was going." She nodded to Jim and Red, then turned to walk away.

Jim glanced at Red and grinned. Could it really be this easy?

"We can share, if you don't mind." Jim couldn't let her get away.

"I would not mind, but—" She wiped her eyes with her handkerchief.

"Oh my, are you crying?" Red reached for the woman's arm to help her sit. Jim stared as Red sat next to the young woman. "Perhaps we could be of assistance."

Jim shoved his hands in his pockets and nodded. Red had said the perfect thing, and Jim wanted to fist bump him, like he might know what that was. Red-faced the young woman. Jim shook his head. She had the rich brunette hair and warm brown eyes of Grandma Stewart. Her rosy complexion held Red captive.

Were the names reappearing as they spoke? Elise's eyes were bright but red-rimmed and puffy. Why had she been crying? Jim gazed down the park and took a step away from the couple on the bench. The air was fresh and sweet, and Red was falling under the spell of Great-great-grandmother. He'd be home before dinner if Carol would ever forgive him.

"I don't know what's gotten into me, crying in front of perfect strangers. I'm sure you two gentlemen have more pressing business." She wadded her handkerchief in her hand and dabbed at her eyes.

Red placed a hand on her shoulder. Jim cleared his throat, and Red jumped. He glanced at Jim as though seeing him for the first time that day.

Jim folded the rim of his hat in his fingers. "We do have pressing business, my friend."

Red nodded. "Yes. Right. Uh, business."

"Of course." Elise rose from the bench, but Red took her hand and she sat.

"I know we just met, but I must ask. Would you like to accompany me for tea sometime?" Red's face turned scarlet.

"Yes. That would be—" A grin spread across her face. "But you have business now, surely. We could make it another time, perhaps. Do you have a business card? For your line of work, I mean. What is your—"

Red handed her his card. He opened and shut his mouth like a big mouth bass on the hook. Jim shook his head and cleared his throat. "We are fathers in the park looking for our three young girls."

Elise frowned. "Are they lost?"

She shifted her gaze up and down the street, and Jim's stomach lurched. That wasn't creepy at all. Was she looking for which way to run? Had he scared her?

"Yes, and one of them is Jim's daughter," Red said.

"Red." Jim frowned at Red, but it was too late. There was no stopping Red now.

"How rude of us. Let me introduce myself." Red stood and bowed to the young woman. "I am Michael McClusky, and this gentleman is my associate Mr. James Stewart. We are auditors for the Portland Trust and Savings."

Well, that was kind of true. At least he hadn't told her they were Secret Service agents. *Oh, what tangled webs we weave—*

He clenched his fists and made a curt bow to the woman. His mind raced. How did he stop Red from scaring her away?

"My name is Elise Meyer. What is your daughter's name?"

"Sam," Red said.

"Then I may have some news for you and two other girls." Elise glanced up at Jim.

Jim froze. He clapped his mouth shut and sank onto the bench next to Red. "Do you know where Sam is?"

"Do not interrupt, Jim. Do go on." Red took Elise's hand in his.

"They are at my grandmother's house. Two errand boys rescued them from the tunnels." Elise batted her eyelashes at Red but didn't remove her hand from his.

This romance thing was working too well. Jim needed them to fall in love, but he couldn't ignore the only lead he had to his daughter. Red stared at her brunette hair shining around her head like a halo, his eyes twinkling. Jim nudged Red.

"Your grandmother's, you say?" Red stuttered. "What are the other girls' names?"

"Nicole and Henri." Elise gasped and clamped her eyes shut. She stood and scanned up and down the Park Blocks again.

Was she looking for someone? She peeped at Red who rose to stand by her. Something had happened, but what? She seemed wary, and Red's focus had shifted from Elise to business.

"Henri? Boy or girl?" Red frowned at Elise.

"Girl." Elise put a hand to her chest.

Jim cleared his throat and forced a smile. "Where

are they?" Time was ticking, and he had to find Sam before Elise bolted or Mr. Stickel found her.

"They are at my grandmother's—"

"You must take us there immediately." Red scrunched his hat in his hand.

"What my friend means is we would be forever in your debt if you would take us to them." Jim made an exaggerated bow.

Elise stared from Jim to Red but clasped her hands in her lap and lowered her eyes. She bit her lip, then glanced first at Red then at Jim more closely. What did she see? Two well dressed, respectable businessmen, but the love spell was wearing off. What should he do?

Her lips pressed together; she stared across the street. Jim glanced in the direction of her gaze at the tall spire of a church.

"I will take you to them, but first I must stop by the church." She glanced up and down the street again. She wasn't comfortable with them yet.

"Church?" A knot settled in his stomach like a stone. Was this a trick?

"Of course." Red shot a frown at Jim. "We will wait for you. Then you can take us to your grandmother's."

Jim followed Elise across the street to a brick church, through a carved oak door. Candles glowed a yellow light against a far wall. He let his eyes adjust as he ran his fingers over his stubbled chin. Sam was foremost in his mind, and this was taking too long. Jim squinted in the dim light of the church. Elise glided down the aisle with her hands folded in front of her. She slid into a pew and bowed her head as Red and Jim took a pew behind her. When she stood, so did Jim.

"Excuse me gentlemen, I must deliver a message to

our pastor. Then we can go."

Red nodded, gazing into Elise's eyes. She rose and walked down the side aisle and ducked into a doorway to the left of the altar.

"I like a church-going woman." Red sighed and stared at the doorway through which Elise had disappeared.

"What about our mission?" Jim kept his attention on the door. What was taking her so long?

"I was trying to be polite." Red hung his head. "Besides she said the girls were at her grandmother's house." Red turned and gazed at Jim a furrow wrinkling his brow.

"I understand, Red. I do, but—"

Red sniffed and looked at his hands. "She had the look of an angel, did she not?"

"You really like her, don't you?"

Red cleared his throat. "I—"

The door clicked shut. Jim jumped to his feet. "This is taking too long."

Red ran to the door where Elise had disappeared and yanked it open. "It opens to the street. Jim, she's gone."

Jim ran to the door, as Red rushed into the street.

"I don't see her." Red turned in circles as he gazed in all directions. "I do not know what came over me."

"She knows where the girls are." Jim searched the street and threw his hands in the air. "Our only lead, and we lost her."

"I was clearly not thinking. It was her eyes, her pink lips, her hair." Red dropped his chin to his chest and sighed. "Henri."

"She must have gone into that neighborhood." Jim pointed to a street sign. "Jefferson Street. Come on." He ran down the sidewalk, Red jogging behind him. Tall trees shaded the streets and dulled the echo of their pounding feet.

****

"Wasn't that Elise Meyer?" Paul stepped out from behind a tree trunk.

"Yep." Will grabbed the bike he'd leaned against the tree trunk.

Paul stared after the two men. "Do you think they are after her?"

"Yep. She looked scared."

"What 'cha say we follow those yahoos and see what they are up to." Paul grabbed his bike and pushed off.

"Yep." Will pedaled to catch up with his brother.

They glided down Jefferson Street side by side as the men turned onto Grandma Meyer's street. They scanned each driveway and house porch but ran past Grandma's driveway.

"We better get to Grandma's quick." Paul stood and pedaled hard.

"Yep." Will raced behind his brother.

Chapter 16

Elise's Return

The front door slammed, and Elise rushed into the library. Sam perched on the edge of the couch. Strands of Elise's hair had drifted in curls around her face and sweat beaded on her brow.

"You are returned." Grandma held out her hands, and Elise stumbled toward her.

"Oh, Grandmother." Elise knelt before her, still gasping from her run.

Bertha hovered at the door with a platter in her hands. The scent of cookies filled the house. She placed the platter on a table and sat in her chair. Would Elise never speak?

Elise cleared her throat. "There were two men."

"Two men? You were going to the park to think, not find men. What men did you find?"

"When I got to the Park, I was crying, and I rushed to a bench and ran into a tall man with red hair and hazel eyes." She bit her bottom lip and glanced at Sam. "I may have put the girls in danger."

Sam jumped to her feet. "You—"

Henri rose from her seat. "Red hair?" Her eyes were wide, and her face paled.

"Girls, please." Grandma clicked her tongue.

The grandfather clock in the entry chimed four.

"It was as though I'd known him all my life, but I'd only just met him for heaven's sake. I thought I could trust him, and then he said he worked for the bank. What was I thinking?"

Sam rubbed the frown lines from her forehead. What did this have to do with anything? They needed to find out how to stop Mr. Stickel and use the bricks to get home.

Grandma patted her hand. "Go on."

Elise swallowed. "Mr. McClusky said they are looking for three girls."

Bertha clattered her teacup in its saucer, and Henri jumped to her feet. "Papa?"

Sam grabbed Nicole's hand. They were here? Were they coming for them?

"Who were they?" Grandma asked.

"Red and Big Jim."

Nicole gasped, as Sam gripped her hand harder. They were running out of time.

"When they told me they were auditors for the Portland Trust and Savings, I knew they were working for Mr. Stickel. Oh, what have I done?"

Sam glanced at Nicole who clutched her arm. Her eyes were so wide, they looked like saucers in her tiny face.

"So, I led them into the church on the pretext that I had to speak with the pastor. I left them sitting in a pew as I ran out the side door, then home as quickly as I could."

"Let's hope they did not follow you into this neighborhood, but even if they knock on every door, they'll never find you, we will not acknowledge that we know you."

A knock on the back door startled them all.

"Grandma," someone called from the porch.

"It's Paul." Grandma nodded to Bertha, and Bertha left the library.

"In here." Bertha led Paul and Will into the library.

Sam jumped to her feet. At least it wasn't Mr. Stickel.

"Ladies." Paul tipped his hat.

Henri blushed. Sam glanced from one to the other. Was Paul turning red too? Were they—

Grandma smiled at Paul. "Tell us the news."

"We followed two men in suits." Paul twisted his hat.

"They followed Elise from the church into the neighborhood." Will planted his feet and held his hat in his hands.

"That means…"

Sam gasped. "That means Red and Big Jim might find us, and if they do, then Mr. Stickel can."

Nicole and Henri sat silent and still.

"We saw you talking to some men and didn't think much about it. Then we saw you lead them into the church, which seemed odd to us, so we followed. Then we saw you run out the side door of the church and down the street toward Grandma's house, so we waited to see what the men would do. They followed you."

"We followed them, but they ran right past the house." Will sniffed and nodded.

"Tell me this. Did you see Mr. Stickel?" Grandma peered at the boys like a bird waiting for crumbs. Elise clasped her hands to her chest.

"Yes."

"Where?"

"In the tunnels. He was arguing with a woman, and she sounded angry."

"What about Frederick?" The tone in Grandma's voice became tense.

"Freddie can take care of himself," Bertha said. "You baby him. Let him figure this one out on his own."

"Oh, Bertha," Grandma said.

****

Jim paced back and forth on the road, letting his heart rate return to normal. Tall trees lined this street just like the Park Blocks, but houses were set deep into landscaped lots with flower beds, lawns, and shrubs. With dismay, Jim scanned the long block. The yards were huge and the houses spaced far apart. Finding the right one would take forever. "I don't see Miss Meyer anywhere."

"She could not have run this far without us seeing her. She must have ducked into one of the houses that we have already passed."

Inhaling the sweet air, he noticed how quiet it was, a much different neighborhood than Nihonmachi, with its noisy vendors speaking Japanese and English, and the smell of fish and horse dung in the streets. Was Sam in one of these houses, so close? Jim sighed, clenching and unclenching his fists as Red wiped his brow his shoulders sagging.

"We lost her." Red stared at the houses in the distance.

"Henri?"

"Yes, Henri, but also...Elise." Red stared at the empty street the only sound the bird song that filtered down from the branches.

"Come on, buddy, let's go back to the park. We

can't knock on every door, and even if we did, her grandmother wouldn't tell two strange men if she lived there. We need a new plan." Jim took a step up the hill and looked back. "Are you coming?"

"Certainly." Red balled the handkerchief in his large hands. "You lead the way. I'll follow. I need a few minutes to sort out my thoughts."

Red's downcast eyes and shuffling pace encouraged Jim. This part of his mission, at least, was successful. He had to focus on the positive, or he'd lose himself to the chaos of worry.

Two boys on bikes pulled onto the street from one of the driveways. Jim stopped.

"Red, those boys might know something." Jim ran after the boys. Could they be the key to finding Sam?

The bigger boy glanced over his shoulder and stood on his pedals. "Hurry, Will." They picked up speed as they pedaled up the hill, and Jim lagged, his fists clenched. Who was he kidding? He skidded to a stop, and panting, watched as they skidded around a corner and sped into the park.

"They came from a house. Which one?" Red squinted down 12th."

"There." Jim pointed.

"That hedge row?" Red ran to the spot and stopped. "There are two driveways."

"Of course, there are." Aunt Elise had warned him about pitfalls. But did it have to be this difficult?

"I'll take this house, and you can take that one." Red's words came between gasps. He glanced from one house to the other, both white manors, one white with black trim, and the other yellow with green.

"What? Knock at both? Look at us." Jim pulled his

hat off his head and wiped the sweat from his brow. "No one's going to open their door to us. Not looking like this."

Red nodded. "You're right. There's a fountain in the park. A quick wipe down, and we can come back and try again."

Jim nodded. Red was back and logical as ever. "Right." He nodded glaring at the green trim. Was Sam in there? Was she safe?

"Number 377." Red wrote and slipped the pad in his jacket pocket.

****

The sun blazed down, but the lush trees on Park Avenue sheltered the park from the full brunt of the heat. It was noon, lunchtime, so the park was almost deserted. By the time he found a fountain, a calm had settled over him, and his heart rate had slowed.

He dipped his hands in the fountain and splashed his face. The dry heat began to evaporate the water on his face and hands almost before he could wipe them. He pulled a comb from his pocket and ran it through his hair one last time.

"How do I look? Should I wear my hat?"

"Yes, to the hat. Your face looks a bit ruddy, but that is to be expected in this heat. How is my appearance?" Red donned his own hat.

"Like a respectable businessman walking home for lunch. Shall we?"

"Too bad we could not apprehend those boys. They know where the girls are, I am certain of it." Red slapped the back of one hand in the palm of the other. It was a mannerism his grandfather performed when he was frustrated. So, this is where it came from. Jim grinned.

"I agree. Too bad we lost Elise. You two could have had a nice stroll around the block."

Red glared at Jim and punched him in the shoulder. Jim liked this man. It was hard to think of him as his great-great-grandfather. It felt bizarre to tease him about the woman who would become one of the Greats. Yet the satisfaction at getting Red and Elise together left him confident. He was close to saving his family.

"Hey, Jim." Red stopped and grabbed Jim by the arm, pointing to a culvert that ran into the hillside. "Look."

A cold chill ran through Jim as an older man with thinning white hair emerged into the sunlight. He wore a black pin-striped suit with cuffed slacks and a white handkerchief in the left breast pocket. As he walked out of the culvert and scrambled up the steep bank to the park, Jim noticed mud stains around his pants' bottoms.

"Stickel?" He glared at the person responsible for the disappearing names. All his hard work would turn to ash if Stickel got Sam before he did.

Stickel scanned the block. Jim walked over to the shade of a building and leaned against it. Red placed his hand on the wall and nodded at Jim as if in friendly conversation. Jim pulled his hat down and tilted his head to keep Stickel in sight. Stickel brushed the dust off his suit then marched down Park Avenue and turned onto Jefferson. A shudder shook Jim's frame. Pushing away from the wall, Jim started down the hill as Stickel turned a corner.

"Did he turn down 12th?" Red jogged to catch up to Jim. "377 is on that street."

"Yes, it is. He's not going to his own house. He's

going to Elise's. Come on. If we can catch him, we may be able to solve this embezzlement case today." Jim took off after Stickel. He clenched his fists and kept his pace to a brisk walk. He couldn't give himself away or Sam was lost.

"Do you think he's after Miss Meyer too?" Red asked. "She said the girls were at her grandmother's."

"I hope not, for her sake."

Jim jogged to the corner of Park Avenue and Jefferson Street. Stickel marched down the street. "Come on, we can't lose him." Jim picked up his pace

Stickel glanced at each house as he walked down the tree-lined streets.

"I don't think he knows where he's going," Red said.

"Shhh." Jim stopped and sniffed the air. "Man, do you smell that? Snickerdoodles."

"He knows right where he's going." Red moved carefully around the hedge as Stickel knocked on the front door of 377.

Jim stopped behind and crouched beside him. He had a perfect view of the three-story house as he peered over Red's shoulder. The double oak doors stood like sentinels closed to all evil, yet evil stood there knocking.

Red shook his head. "It is as though he wants to get caught."

"He's not thinking straight. He must be desperate, and the girls must be in that house." Jim ducked as someone opened the door.

An older woman with white hair opened the door. "Yes?" The woman gasped. "Charles? I thought you'd been murdered."

"You know I'm not dead, so don't play games with

me. Paul and Will delivered my letter to you, and I know it. Freddie's life depends on your cooperation. Now let me in."

Jim froze as Stickel pushed past the older woman and stomped into the house. How did they know him?

Chapter 17

The Back Stairs

Bertha gasped. She slipped the key into her pocket and the book back on the shelf then motioned for Sam to follow her. Henri helped Nicole and they scurried through a back door from the library to the kitchen. Bertha pointed out a door in the corner by the pantry then turned to walk back to the library. Sam jumped at the sound of Mr. Stickel's voice. How had he found them?

Sam opened the door. Stairs rose to the second story. Henri helped Nicole, and Sam led them up the back stairs. Sam raced to the second floor and stopped at a small landing. There were two doors. She paused.

Nicole nudged her shoulder. "Choose one already."

Leave it to Nicole. Her hand shaking, Sam clasped the knob to the one on the right. It opened without a sound.

"It's the room Bertha brought us to when we first arrived." Henri pushed past Sam with Nicole. Across the room, another door stood open. Henri tiptoed to the open door. Stickel's muffled voice filtered up from the parlor.

"A crystal doorknob?" Nicole clasped it and turned. "Why didn't I notice that before."

"Shhh." Henri held her finger to her lips and closed the door until it was open a crack.

Stickel's voice echoed from the parlor, and Sam

shrank back into Nicole.

"…those girls today, or I'll…"

Henri gasped. Sam and Nicole leaned over her shoulder.

"Now what do we do?" Henri backed into the room. Her lips quivered.

"It'll be okay." Sam put her arm around Henri's shoulder. "We'll think of something."

"I thought we'd be safe here." Henri's shoulders shook.

"Me too," Nicole whispered.

Sam glanced at the door. Stickel wasn't supposed to find them here. She'd trusted Paul and Will. Did Stickel find them too?

"I thought I could find my father. How stupid."

"I thought Grandma would help us go home." Nicole shook her head.

Grandma's voice came through the register. "…won't let you touch a hair on their…"

Sam reached for Henri and gripped her shoulder. "Don't give up yet. Grandma will help us."

Henri brushed her eyes with the back of her hand. "You are right. Grandma will find a way. This is no time to cry."

"That's the spirit," Sam whispered. "Now we need a plan."

"No more plans." Nicole placed her hands over her ears. "Your plans get us into more trouble."

"I have an idea." Henri rushed across the room to the door that led to the kitchen stairs. She pulled it open and glanced over her shoulder for them to follow. Sam took Nicole's hand and they rushed after her onto the small landing. Henri crossed the small space and opened the door that they hadn't taken. It revealed another set of narrow stairs.

Henri glanced at Sam. "They lead to the attic. Let's go."

Sam turned to Nicole. "How's your ankle?"

Nicole put her arm over Sam's shoulder and grabbed the banister. "Just go."

Henri waited at the top of the stairs. She reached out her hand to turn the knob but hesitated. "Did anyone close the door with the crystal knob?"

"No." The hair stood on Sam's neck. "Why?"

"Stickel will follow the open doors all the way to this attic and find us."

"Now you tell us." Nicole wilted against Sam.

Henri opened the door and light filled the stairwell.

Sam stumbled into the bright room. Color filled the space from the patchwork quilt to the Tuscan yellow paint on the walls. "This is someone's bedroom." The sun's heat radiated through the roof. "I can see the park and the buildings downtown."

"Look at all the needlework." Henri held up a pillow with red roses embroidered in a corner. "This must be Bertha's room."

"Shh. I hear voices." Nicole listened at the heat register. "We can't stay here."

Sam crouched beside Nicole. "It's Grandma."

"Charles, listen to me." Grandma was pleading with him, but it wasn't working.

"...won't get away this time."

"Is this room haunted?" Nicole huddled in a corner, rubbing her ankle.

Henri peered out the window. "We can't escape onto the roof. It's too steep."

"Voices really carry in this old house." Sam scanned the garret ceiling, and the flowered wallpaper.

Henri shook her head and frowned at Sam. "Old? This house? Why, it's new."

"Old, new, who cares? How are we hearing them?" Sam glared at Henri.

"The boiler pumps hot water through the radiators, but these registers allow heat to fill the rooms throughout the house. It stands to reason that the registers also carry sound." Henri placed a hand on the wrought iron grate in the floor. It's like the ones in the library and the kitchen.

"How do you know this?" Nicole tilted her head her eyebrows raised.

"My grandparents built a home just like this in Salem, and I used to play games with my cousins. We'd call through the registers."

Sam rubbed her chin. "So, these are on every floor in every room?"

"They are."

"Wait. I can't hear them anymore," Nicole whispered. "We need to get out of here before Stickel comes." Nicole stood.

Sam tiptoed onto the stairs. "I have an idea. Quick. We—"

Henri gasped. "The cellar. Are you—"

"I am." Sam grinned at Henri. "To the cellar."

"Not another underground." Nicole pulled back.

Henri took Nicole's arm and pulled it over her shoulder. "We have no choice."

Sam nodded. "We're going down."

****

The house at 377 stood three stories tall, sunshine gleaming off every window, even the little rectangular windows of the basement. There was a door at the side of the house for coal deliveries. This house had a boiler. Jim pulled his hat down to shade his eyes from the sun. A scent of lavender floated on the breeze, and Jim glanced at the porch. What was he missing? This all seemed so peaceful, but Sam must be in there.

Jim stepped into the driveway. "This has to be the house, and we can't wait any longer."

"Agreed." Red jogged after Jim down the driveway to the backdoor.

Jim stopped on the back porch and took off his hat. Bertha opened the door as Jim raised his hand to knock. He stepped back.

"Yes?" Bertha glared from Jim to Red."

"I'm—"

"It doesn't matter." Bertha stood to the side and waved them in. "I know why you are here."

Jim rushed into the kitchen his heart racing. Where was Sam? Bertha nodded to Red who removed his hat. "Where—"

"He's headed upstairs with Delores." Bertha nodded to a doorway in the back corner beside a pantry.

Elise rushed into the kitchen and gasped. "I thought I heard your voice Red, I mean, Mr. McClusky." Elise flew to Red's side. "I am so very sorry I left you in the church."

Red took her hand in his. "You were trying to protect the girls, but you can trust us. You know that now, right?"

Jim clenched his teeth. If these two were courting, he had to let them have their moment, but couldn't they hurry?

She sobbed and clutched his hands. "He has

Grandma and the girls."

Bertha put a hand on Elise's shoulder. "We don't know that."

Elise brushed her hand away. "We don't, but those girls are in the house somewhere and so is Charles. If he finds—"

"That settles it." Jim clenched his teeth and strode across the kitchen. He yanked open the door. "Let's get him."

Red nodded and followed Jim. They took the stairs two at a time. Jim's heart pounded against his ribs. Sam had to be okay.

"Is that you, Freddie?" A form stood on the steps, and Jim stopped. An elderly woman clutched the banister.

"Mrs. Meyer?" Jim stopped, gripping the railing.

"You're not Freddie."

The hair on the back of his neck rose as she brushed passed him on the narrow stairs.

"Wait. Where are the girls?" Ice ran through his veins.

Grandma didn't respond. He glanced at Red, who shrugged and followed her down the stairs. She staggered into the kitchen. Where were the girls? In trouble somewhere in this house. What did he do now?

"Grandmother." Elise ran to her.

"Charles has them."

Elise gasped. Jim grabbed the door frame as his knees wobbled, and he stumbled. Red grabbed his elbow to steady him. The names seemed to fade before his eyes. His mission was a failure and all because of a madman.

"What has happened?" Red glanced from Grandma to Elise. "Where's Henri?"

Jim shook his head. "Stickel can't have the girls." He couldn't be too late. "How did Stickel do it?"

Red slumped against a counter as Elise helped Grandma to a chair at the table. How would he ever save Sam now? She must be terrified. How did he tell Aunt El—

Jim scratched his head glancing at the stairs. "Wait a minute. If Stickel has the girls, why isn't there yelling?"

Red pushed away from the counter. "There should be sounds of a struggle or something, right?" A grin spread across Red's face, and he nodded.

"That means there is still a chance." Jim dashed to the stairs but skidded to a stop.

Stickel stood in the doorway pointing a gun at him.

"What have you done with the girls?" Red clenched his fists, shaking one at Stickel.

Jim grabbed his arm. He should let Red do it, clasp his fingers around Stickel's throat, but he didn't have the girls.

"What girls?" Stickel pushed past Red and stepped into the kitchen.

"No." Grandma jumped to her feet.

Stickel waved the gun. "Over there with the others if you don't mind."

"If you touched one hair on—" Red glared at Stickel who waved the pistol at him.

Jim winced. "Let's all try to remain calm." He held his hands out, and Red's nostrils flared. He had to stop Red from rushing Stickel, or Stickel from shooting Red? He gripped Red's arm.

"Yes, Red, let's not be rash." Stickel trained the gun on Red's chest.

No, no, no. Jim glanced at the stairs behind Stickel. If Stickel had killed the girls there, would have been shots. If Red died, all the names would disappear, and so would he, and—

"You are mad," Red said

"Yes, I am quite angry." Stickel swung around and waved the gun at Bertha. "Now, call me a carriage. I have to get to the Lucky Star."

"I need you to know," Bertha stood and glared at him, "that I never liked you, Charlie." Mr. Stickel winced as she walked to a black phone hanging on the wall. She turned the crank. "Hello, Mabel. Yes, it's Bertha. It is going to be another hot one."

Mr. Stickel shook the gun at her. "Order the carriage."

"Listen, Mable, I'm in a rush here. Portland Carriage, please. Thanks, Dear."

Bertha held the phone in her hand as Mr. Stickel smirked. Jim clenched his jaw and hissed a sigh through his teeth. He'd need a miracle to fix this mess.

"No funny business." Mr. Stickel shifted the gun toward Jim and Red.

He's insane. Jim wanted to wipe that smirk off Stickel's face. He glared at the wrinkles in Stickel's slacks and the dirt smudges on his shirt collar. He and Red could easily overpower him, but if someone got shot...

He couldn't risk it.

"Hello, Portland Carriage? Yes, we need a car at 377 and Jackson. Yes. As soon as you can." Bertha slammed the receiver in the cradle.

"Why are you doing this, Charles? Your mother would be so disappointed in you." Grandma wrung her hands.

Stickel chuckled. "Mother's dead. No one can stop me now." He grinned and waved the gun through the air.

Jim tightened his fists. Stickel handled the gun like a toy. If he could somehow get that gun from him...

Red nudged him and motioned toward the gun. Stickel didn't have his finger on the trigger. How had he missed that? Jim tensed and focused on the gun. This was his chance.

"ooooooooooo."

Jim froze and cocked his head.

"Chaaaarrrrlllllesssss,"

Mr. Stickel's mouth dropped open. The gun dropped and hung limp at his side. He scanned the floor and ceiling.

Jim glanced at Grandma. Elise and Bertha sat perched on the edge of their seats. Stickel staggered, gazing into the dark corners of the kitchen. Did the girls escape? Were they doing this? If so, it was pure genius.

Stickel swung the gun at the women with a wobble. "W-w-w-e sh-sh-should wait for the carriage in the p-p-parlor."

Grandma stood, and Jim and Red fell in line behind Elise, Bertha, and Grandma as they marched single file through the dining room and into the parlor. Bertha glanced back at Jim, a smile lifting the corner of her lips.

"What was that?" Red whispered as they followed the women into the parlor.

Jim shook his head.

"No talking." Stickel jabbed the gun in Jim's back.

Jim frowned at Stickel and strode to the fireplace as the women settled on the couch. Stickel glanced into the foyer, sweat dripping down his cheeks. He seemed to be shrinking, as he gripped the gun handle with shaking hands.

"Chaaaarrrrllllesssss…Chaaaarrrrllllesssss…I'm so disappointed in you,

Chaaaarrrrllllesssss."

Goosebumps rose on Jim's arms. Who was doing this? Red moved to stand in front of Elise, using his body as a shield.

Stickel's eyes bulged. He waved the gun in all directions, searching for the source. "M-m-m-mother?" He darted a glance from one side of the room to the other. "M-m-m-mother, is that you?"

The eerie voice was pushing Stickel over the edge of sanity, but would that work for or against them?

"Chaaaarrrrllllesssss."

The voice echoed louder. It rumbled through the entire house, from the kitchen to the parlor and through the foyer.

Stickel clutched the gun and pointed it at the ceiling. "I won't go back to the bank. I won't go, I tell you." He fired the gun, and plaster exploded falling to the floor. Elise screamed as dust filled the air.

Stickel spun, scrambled through the foyer and out the front door. He clattered down the steps, the screen door slamming behind him. Jim started after him.

Red blinked. "He has lost his mind."

Bertha glared at Jim. "He's headed back to the tunnels."

"Right." Jim dashed out the door. If he didn't catch Stickel this time—

Chapter 18

The Ghosts

The boiler sat squat and black in the center of the cellar. Sam knelt by the duct that let heat rise to the rooms. She wiped coal dust off her forehead. Henri brushed coal dust out of her hair and wobbled as she stood. Sam pulled Nicole to a stand and into a hug. Had they convinced Stickel he was being haunted? If they didn't, he was still up there waiting for them. She clung to Nicole.

Henri wrapped her arms around Sam and Nicole, and Sam pulled her into the embrace. This running-for-one's-life business was exhausting.

Henri pulled away. "Did you hear that? The front door just slammed. He left the house."

"We did it." Sam grinned.

"But who shot the gun?" Nicole frowned.

"Listen." Henri held a finger to her lips. "Grandma's speaking."

Sam strained to make out the muffled voice.

"Are they in the cellar then? They are our only hope."

"That's Bertha." Henri nodded.

"Let's find some ghosts, shall we?"

"That's Grandma." Nicole squeezed Sam's hand.

"Care to place a little wager?"

Bertha chuckled. "Keep your money. We'd be betting on the same horse.'

"Was it the girls?" Elise's soft voice echoed in the ductwork.

"What are we waiting for?" Sam raced for the stairs.

Sam rushed into the parlor. Elise gasped, and Sam held out a hand to steady her. She pulled back. Her hands were covered in coal dust. She must look like a ghost.

"Never mind the dirt." Grandma nodded. "I knew it was you as soon as the first moan echoed through the register. Brilliant."

Bertha stood beaming behind Grandma. "Mr. Stickel believed it was his dead mother coming back from the grave. Well done, girls."

Henri and Nicole shuffled into the parlor.

"Henri."

"Father?" Henri froze. Red pulled his daughter into his arms, and she clung to him, tears welling in her eyes.

"Father, I was so afraid you…"

Red rocked her in a tight embrace, and she couldn't finish what she was going to say—dead. A small shiver ran down Sam's spine. They all needed some good news after all the disappearances, suspected shanghaies, and hiding. Red released Henri and held her at arm's length, his eyes were red-rimmed. A thick warmth spread through Sam's chest. She missed her own father. Wasn't that why she was here? But how could she ever get back to him now? Didn't they need Stickel to use the bricks?

"So, it worked?" Nicole blinked in the bright light of the parlor.

"He ran out of here as though he'd heard a ghost." Grandma took Sam's hand in her own, smiling at her. "Big Jim chased after him. Portland will be much safer with him behind bars, and the Portland Trust and Savings Bank will hopefully recover their money."

"I hope so too, but—" Sam gripped Grandma's hand.

"I hope they catch that bastard." Nicole rubbed her ankle.

"Nicole." Grandma shook her head, but her lips twitched into a grin.

Sam sighed. Nicole was only here because of her. She had touched the bricks, trying to get her father back…like Henri did, but Henri got her wish.

Bertha tapped her watch. "I hate to interrupt, but the book was very clear. We only have until midnight. Then whatever magic was placed on the bricks expires, so we should finish this in the library."

Grandma squeezed Sam's hand. "She's right."

They all shuffled into the library, and Nicole sneezed. Book dust always got to her. Grandma cleared her throat, her hand on the velvet book beside her.

"Tell us why you used the bricks."

Sam swallowed. The why was going to sound so stupid. "Mom and Dad fought, and Dad left. It had been a week, and I missed him so much it hurt. It got worse on my birthday. He always made me birthday waffles, and I wanted to get him back." She shrugged.

"And when is your birthday, dear." Grandma held her hands clasped in her lap.

"July 7th." What did this have to do with anything?

"That's tomorrow."

"Oh." Sam stared at Grandma. "So, the tour hasn't happened yet?"

"Let her speak, Delores." Bertha patted Grandma's shoulder. Grandma nodded.

"We were on the tour when I smelled lavender. At first, I thought it was the key in my pocket that had caused the fight. We were in the room with the bricks, and I could see them glow. When the group left, I stayed behind. It was the scent of lavender that drew me to them."

"I see. So, you smelled the lavender and touched the bricks then found yourself here in 1901." Grandma glanced at Bertha whose face was white and grim. She nodded to Sam. "Anything else?"

Sam glared at Nicole. Now she decides to keep her mouth shut. Nicole shook her head, and Sam sighed. "The bricks started to glow when the guide was telling us a story about Big Jim and Red McClusky murdering—"

"That is a lie." Red shook his head.

Henri glanced up at her father and put her hand on his arm. "The world will soon know the truth."

Grandma held up her hand. "Please." She glared at Red then turned back to Sam. "What else."

"The bricks glowed, and as the group left the room, I stayed behind so I could test my theory, and—"

"I tried to stop her." Nicole hobbled forward but plopped down in a chair.

"So, Nicole had contact with you when you touched the bricks?" Elise frowned.

A shiver ran down Sam's back. "Yes. I placed my hand flat on the bricks, like this." Sam pressed her hand on the fireplace. "I felt the air being sucked from my lungs then we were in the Lucky Star stockroom. That's where Henri found us."

Grandma tapped her finger on the book, her eyes mere slits. "Did you say anything before you touched the bricks?"

"I don't think so. Did I, Nicole?"

"I remember what *I* said." Nicole frowned at Sam. " 'Don't touch them.' But did she listen? Nooooo."

Grandma's eyes glittered as she smiled at Nicole. "But she did touch them, and here you are." She sighed. "This is all Charles's fault." Grandma wadded her handkerchief in her hands.

"My mission is still to apprehend Mr. Stickel." Red's chest was heaving. "He could have hurt you girls." He placed a hand on Henri's cheek and cleared his throat. "Big Jim will be returning with Stickel any time now, and we will need to transport him to the Portland jail." Red tucked Henri under his arm.

Bertha nodded. "I'll call another carriage."

"Did that book say anything about how the bricks work?" Sam asked.

Grandma gazed at Sam. "You may not believe this, but Bertha will find out how those bricks work."

A knock at the front door echoed through the foyer.

****

Frederick sat in a wooden chair his hands tied behind his back. Every corner in the room was dark, which meant he was still in the tunnels. A gas lamp on the wall illuminated a table in the center of the room. He looked into the mirror on the wall and saw the bags under his eyes and the brilliant purple bruise on his cheekbone. At least he felt better than he looked.

"This is the last time I'm going to ask you, Meyer. Where did Stickel go?" Mr. Lawrence's eyebrows bushed over his eyes and his hair stuck out in black tufts around his ears. Freddie wanted to laugh, but the grin on Mr. Lawrence's face was more frightening than the ropes that bound him to the chair. He glanced at his swollen lip in the mirror. The last thing he needed was another punch in the face. That hurt.

Freddie closed his eyes. The throb in his cheekbone kept time with his pulse. If only he'd run faster. He would be with Archie on his way home, instead of sitting here tied to a chair with a man who didn't believe a word he said.

He hung his head. What would his grandmother do when she found out his part in all of this? But if she didn't find out, he would disappear out to sea.

Sweat ran down the side of his face. He wanted to itch it and struggled against the rope. He sighed and sank back into the chair. No one was coming. He sobbed. "Elise, what have we done."

****

A bike bell ringing outside floated into the open window on the breeze. Red strode across the room. "I'll answer it, Bertha."

Red opened the door, and a scream filled the air. He dragged a man into the library behind him. Sam clutched her chest and stared at Archie as Red towered over him. It was the tour guide. How was he here? He glowered at Red. A thump brought Bertha to her feet. She scurried across the room and bent over Elise.

Bertha patted Elise's cheek. Elise opened her eyes, and Bertha helped her to a chair. She gasped and pointed at Archie as if he were a ghost. Sam grabbed Nicole's hand. He must have used the bricks, but how?

"What are you doing at this house?" Red shook Archie by the collar until his teeth chattered.

Nicole leaned toward Sam. "I knew there was something creepy about him."

Archie stared at Red with his unblinking amber eyes, a red welt forming on his left cheekbone. Red shook him again, and Archie clung to Red's arm, as he hung there like a rag doll.

Elise rose from the couch as if in a trance and glided to Red's side. She placed her hand on his shoulder. "Do not hurt him. Please."

"Do not—" Red opened and closed his mouth at a loss for words. "Did not this man work for Mr. Stickel?"

Sam shuddered at the mention of Stickel's name. Archie had a connection to the bricks, but what was it?

"Yes, but that is not his fault, just as activating the bricks is not Freddie's." Elise helped Archie to stand.

Red's frown grew deeper as he hovered over Archie. "Do you have something you want to say, Archibald Pisica?"

"Yes, I do. You may not believe me, but I am here to help you." Archie glanced at Grandma.

Grandma's eyes seemed to be pleading with him, but why? Sam glanced from Grandma to Archie. There was a bond between them, and it had to do with the bricks.

"I came here to warn Grandma." Archie glared at Red. "I know where Freddie is, but we must hurry." He turned his gaze to Grandma.

"Oh, Archie, I knew you'd find him." Grandma clasped her hands together as if in prayer. Sam's stomach lurched, and she swallowed hard.

"So, you admit that you are the rascal who worked for Stickel." Red was like a dog with a bone. He wasn't going to let this go, even if Grandma and Elise begged him to.

Sam's brain whirled. How did Elise know Archie,

and why would Grandma care about him? Red's face turned scarlet, and his eyes close to slits. Was he jealous? Red clenched and unclenched his fists.

"Where did Stickel go?" Red shook his fist at Archie.

"I have no idea where that maniac went, but if we don't hurry, Freddie will sail on the evening tide." Archie squinted at Red.

"There is a carriage on the way." Bertha placed a hand on Grandma's shoulder. "It will be the fastest way to get to Freddie."

Grandma nodded then patted the arm of the couch. "Rest here, Archie."

Archie perched next to Grandma and closed his eyes. She put her hand over his, and he leaned into the fold of the arm and the backrest. Was he another relative?

"Bertha's right. We have to wait for the carriage, but we must also hear out how the bricks were activated?" Grandma pursed her lips and cocked her eyebrow at Elise.

Elise clasped her hands and cleared her throat. "Freddie and I created a spell."

"And you were afraid to tell me. Any anger I may have felt is replaced by fear for Freddie's life. Please, Elise, tell me everything."

Elise sighed. "I will." She shuddered. "I lit the candles while Freddie prepared the bricks."

"Were you and Freddie holding hands?" Grandma leaned forward.

"We were, and Charles placed one of his hands on Freddie's shoulder and one on mine, so we formed a triangle."

"Of course," Grandma said. "A triangle is the strongest shape, and the magic would run equally through all three of you. That would allow Charles to use the spell later. Drat his photographic memory."

Bertha sighed. "He might be crazy, but he is a genius."

Grandma stared at Elise without blinking. "Recite the spell for us, dear."

A tingle ran down Sam's spine. This was it. She clenched her shut and gritted her teeth. What would Elise say?

Elise closed her eyes, and in a monotone recited:
Ancestors we bow on bended knee
And ask you with our loving plea
Awaken portals of ancient rite
With our touch as we alight
Our hands upon these bricks of clay
Transport us through the misty array
to—

"Then Freddie said, '*Seattle,*' where Charles wanted to go." Elise slouched back on the couch like a deflated balloon.

"I see." Grandma took Elise's hands in her own. "Freddie called the power of love, which is what helped activate them. Do you remember the date on which your parents had their accident, and you came to live with me? It was the very day you empowered those bricks. This was no accident."

"So, Charles knew what—" Elise covered her face with her hands.

"He did. He also knew that for this spell to work, he needed a trinity to complete the spell. The first connection is grief that created the bricks, the second is

187

the blood passed down through the family. The third is love." Grandma glanced at Sam. "You have all three as well. That is why the bricks worked for you."

"I don't understand?" Sam stared into space. The scent of lavender filled the room, and she folded her arms across her chest. This was crazy. How would this help her get home?

A small smile twitched the corner of Grandma's mouth. "All I need is a mirror and I can show you."

"A mirror?" Sam stepped back, but Grandma took her by the shoulder and positioned her in the middle of the room.

"Elise, come stand here." She positioned Elise beside Sam.

Nicole gasped. "They look like twins except for Elise's fancy hair and dress."

Chills ran down Sam's spine.

"I did not notice before…" Henri stared from Sam to Elise.

"Grandmother, what are you doing?" Elise tried to pull away, but Grandma held her still and glanced at Archie at the back of the library.

Archie nodded, and Sam gulped. He already knew what Grandma was going to say. His amber eyes blinked twice at Sam, and he smiled as he turned his gaze to Grandma.

Sam's stomach churned. "What?" She stepped away from Elise, unable to look in her eyes. "Do you think we're related?"

Elise stared open-mouthed at her grandmother. "Are we?" Elise put her hands on her head.

"Yes. You must be. If blood is what makes the bricks. If what Bertha read is correct, it is your blood that will get you to your own time."

****

The tunnel ran downhill to the river, and water ran through the tunnel creating puddles and muddy patches. Jim slipped and slid as he raced after Stickel, who had disappeared into the dark. He stopped and cupped a hand to his ear. Footsteps and then a thud echoed from somewhere ahead.

"Damn it." Mr. Stickel's voice echoed through the tunnel.

Jim rushed forward. If he fell too, Stickel might get away. Did he turn here? He followed the light from several candles that illuminated a wide space ahead. Mr. Stickel was mumbling and someone else mumbled back. Jim slowed. What was he running into? There was more than one voice, and they were women, and they were angry. He inched closer.

"You dirty dog. You'll burn in hell for what you do." The speaker held a lantern in one hand, her other a fist ready to strike.

"Girls. They are just girls most of them," another cried.

"You don't understand." Stickel's voice sounded loud and confident. "I'm out of that business now. I'm going to Nome, Alaska to pan for gold."

"You ain't gonna make it to Nome, Alaska, you snake in the grass."

Were they hitting Stickel? Not like he didn't deserve it, but the thuds made him wince, and the rustle of skirts—

If he didn't hurry, he'd have to make multiple arrests, maybe even for murder, and he did not want that.

"Stop. I'm arresting this man for embezzlement."

Jim ran into the fray of women who continued to kick and hit Stickel. "I need him alive so he can stand trial."

"Hornswoggle. Stickel is ours."

"You tell him, Sally," another said.

Jim stared at Stickel in a slick of mud, and eight women surrounding him. They had him pinned down, and up close they were well muscled and tough, but hornswoggle? He couldn't stop a grin from spreading across his face.

Stickel tried to stand but slipped in the mud and rolled onto his stomach as the women continued to take turns kicking him. Jim was torn. Part of him had to enforce the law against violent attacks, but the other part wanted to join in the kicking.

"Stand back ladies." Jim stepped inside the circle of women who glared at Stickel lying at their feet. Stickel, his face and hair matted with mud, and his suit covered in a slick, muddy sheen, glanced from the women to Jim.

"You're finished, Stickel." Jim held his hand out to ward off the women. "I arrest you in the name of the United States Government for embezzlement, racketeering, grand larceny, and other deeds that will reveal themselves at your trial, I'm sure."

"My case will never go to trial, young man." Mr. Stickel wiped the mud from his face. "I will not say one more word without my lawyer."

The women bunched closer, all talking at once.

"Do your job, man."

"This scoundrel must go to jail."

"He has shanghaied men and women."

"Right off the streets and sent them out to sea."

"They ain't never been heard from again."

"We got him right where we want him, girls."

Another woman kicked Mr. Stickel in the side. He fell back into the mud. The circle of women grew tighter. Where'd the other two come from? He pulled his gun from his pocket.

"I said stop." Jim pointed the gun at the ceiling and cocked it.

At sight of the gun, the women backed away. Two in the rear disappeared into the darkness of a side tunnel.

"Ladies." Jim held out his hands. "Arresting him will assure you justice. The Judge will put him away for a hundred years. More importantly, I need him to clear my name and that of my partner for his murder because, as you can plainly see, he ain't dead. Now let me have him."

Jim stood facing the women and after a long moment, they stepped back from Mr. Stickel. Jim let the gun drop to his side. A giddy sense of relief that he didn't have to use it washed over him.

"Save me." Stickel scooted away from the women. "They're crazy. They're insane."

"You could be talking about yourself, you pig-in-a-sty." Sally shook her fist.

The women laughed as Stickel slipped and rolled his face in the mud.

"You resort to name calling, you gutter tramps?" Mr. Stickel's pants came in short bursts as he struggled to gain solid footing and failed.

"Look, Officer." One of the women pointed at Stickel. "This is a bad guy. He tried to kidnap my sister, Sally." She put a hand on Sally's shoulder.

Sally nodded. "We've lost husbands, sons, sisters, and cousins. They just disappeared without a trace, all because of this one man. You don't know what that's like."

Jim looked at Sally and all the women. "Actually, I do." Jim put his gun back in the holster. "I know too well what this man is capable of. My name is Big Jim Stewart, and my partner is Red McClusky—"

One of the women gasped. Another whispered, "The murderers?"

"We're working undercover to apprehend Mr. Charles Stickel for embezzling money, which in turn will shut down his other illegal Portland operations.

Was he convincing them? Silence filled the tunnel, and Jim took that as a good sign. "I'll need you to guard Stickel just like you're doing while I get my partner. We'll return shortly, and I'll get your statements when we return. We need them as testimony to put him away."

Three more women disappeared into the darkness, leaving just three.

"I'll tell you everything I know." Sally stood with her hands on her hips. "Cora?"

"If Sally talks, so will I." Cora swayed, and the lantern she held cast long shadows against the walls and ceiling.

"Me too." A third woman shook her fist. She wore a tattered housedress over her large frame. "When I heard he'd been murdered, I could have spit fire. I wanted to kill him myself. I want to shake your hand, Big Jim."

"Way to speak your peace, Madge." Sally grinned.

Madge held out her hand and Jim took it. Mr. Stickel inched his way out of the candlelight, but Sally stepped on his coat hem, and he rolled into the mud wallow he'd created in his struggles.

Sally slapped her leg. "Where do you think you're going, little piggy?"

Jim grinned. Stickel wasn't going anywhere. Now, where was Red? He ran into the tunnels.

****

A bell ringing on the street in front of Grandma's house jolted Sam. Her stomach grumbled. There would be no time to waste, no time for dinner, not with time ticking down.

"It's our carriage." Red held Archie's arm never taking his gaze off him. "Archie and I will rescue Mr. Meyer and meet you in the tunnels as soon as we can."

Sam gazed out the front window into the street at a horse hitched to a wagon at the end of the driveway. This was a real carriage. She chuckled. Mom would never believe this, but she could never tell her. The horse shook its head rattling the harness.

"Safe trip." Grandma saluted Red, and turning to Bertha, she nodded. "Order another carriage. Quick. We need to arrive at the Lucky Star stockroom before they do." Grandma's firm voice commanded. "Henri?"

"I have the keys." Henri held out the brass ring, and her father pulled her into one last hug, planting a kiss on the top of her head.

Sam hugged her arms tighter, but it didn't make up for the hugs from her mom and dad. This was almost over, and soon Dad would be there to kiss the top of her head.

"I will see you at the Lucky Star." He winked at Elise and a small bow to everyone else. Then he walked out the front door pulling Archie with him.

Grandma stared after him. "Where's my purse and—"

"Right here." Bertha held out a purse the size of a small suitcase.

Grandma took it and reached inside, a gleam shining from her eyes. "Good. We'll need the book. Are you girls ready to go home?"

Chapter 19

Bertha's Story

The stone house across the street from Grandma's glowed like a mystical castle in the evening sun. Grandma Meyer stood on the porch shading her eyes, as a carriage pulled over to the curb in front of the house pulled by two horses. Bertha must have told them how many people in their party. They'd need the extra horsepower.

Grandma rushed down the sidewalk. "Hurry girls, it is already 8:00." She stepped into the carriage. "Driver, to the Lucky Star."

Sam pulled herself into the taxi while Bertha and Henri helped Nicole. Was this her final hour in Portland? She could only hope. The carriage rocked as Elise clambered in beside Grandma.

"Git-up now." The driver shook the reins, and the carriage jerked forward as the horses set off at a brisk trot. A slight breeze rushed through the carriage as they sped down 12th street, stirring the hot July air.

"We'll be there soon, my dears." Grandma pulled a hanky from her purse and dabbed at her temples and chin.

How soon was soon? The horses clopped down the street, but the carriage seemed to move at a snail's pace. Sam could run faster. Why did everything have to move so slowly in 1901?

"We only have four hours." Bertha closed the pocket watch and slipped it back into her pocket.

Elise frowned, and Sam gripped the seat, but it didn't make the carriage go any faster.

"Will you please tell us your plan now, Grandma?" Elise asked.

"First, Bertha must tell us her story." Grandma patted Bertha's hand.

"Why?" Elise was as impatient as Sam.

It seemed so rude and out of character. Sam glanced at Bertha, who scowled out the window as they turned onto Jefferson Street. Nicole placed her hand on Bertha's, and a look of understanding passed between them as though they shared some secret. Nicole did have a way of empathizing with people that Sam didn't, but this seemed like something more.

Nicole held Bertha's hand. "Ever since we met, I've wondered why you hardly ever smile. Does it have something to do with your story?"

Bertha's mouth twitched. She didn't smile, but her eyes sparkled, and Sam realized Bertha was holding back tears.

"My story will be as long as our carriage ride to the Lucky Star, which is anything but a lucky place."

Bertha turned to Nicole, as though the story were for her alone. "As you all know by now, Delores, I mean Grandma, has a soft spot for people in trouble. She has had it since she was a little girl. That's when we met, so long ago now." Bertha smiled at Grandma who nodded.

"She was with her father at the riverfront, where he worked at his shipping company. He delivered logging equipment to Seattle, Alaska, San Francisco, and to mills on the West Coast. Delores would sneak into the tunnels and explore them, especially on hot summer days just like this one."

"Grandmother? In the tunnels?" Elise shook her head. "Why have I never heard this story? I cannot imagine you in those awful tunnels."

"This is why she must tell it. So, you understand what is at stake if we don't succeed." Grandma dabbed at her forehead with her kerchief. "I was quite the tomboy hiking in the forest, riding horses, swimming in the Willamette, but those tunnels. They were so cool in the summertime. I've never tolerated the heat very well. But please, Bertha, continue."

Bertha cleared her throat. "It was July 1961 in Seattle."

"July 1961? Archie mentioned a girl who disappeared around that time." Sam stared at Bertha and scratched her head. "The bricks didn't exist during that time. Did they?"

"Let me tell my story, girl." Bertha frowned at Sam. "The bricks existed in 1961. Freddie and Elise cast their spell in 1901, so by 1961 the bricks had existed for sixty years."

Nicole scratched her head. "But did Seattle have underground tours in 1961?"

"Not tours, but the underground has existed since the 1890s. My father was part of a survey crew preparing for the demolition of some of the old buildings in that area. There was a group fighting to save those old buildings. I'm assuming they were successful if there is an Old Pioneer Underground Tour?"

Nicole nodded. "Yes."

The carriage hit a pothole as the horses trotted down

Park Avenue, the clatter of their hooves echoing off of the apartment buildings and the neighborhood storefronts. Sam shook her head. Was Bertha the girl from Archie's story?

"We'd moved to a new neighborhood, and I was bored and acting like a brat, so my mother sent me to work with my dad." She brushed away stray hairs that had escaped from her bun.

"So, your dad was part of a crew that wanted to tear down the old buildings. The Old Pioneers Square didn't even exist?" Sam's knees wobbled. "So how did you get here?"

"I'm getting to that." Bertha stared at her hands. "I explored the underground rooms and passageways. The old buildings were full of cabinets, signs, and old-fashioned light fixtures. It seemed like garbage to me, but it was a way to stay cool on a hot summer day, just like Delores said. I wandered around as Dad worked until I found a room with some bricks glo—"

"*Déjà vu.*" Sam put a hand to her mouth. "I thought that story of the girl was made up, just something Archie told on the tours."

"He spoke the truth. I touched those bricks and then I was here in Portland. For whatever reason, I went back to 1861 before the bricks existed, which seriously complicated my situation."

The carriage turned onto Salmon Street, and the aroma of freshly baked bread filled the air. Sam's stomach growled.

"At first, I thought I was still in Seattle. I thought I'd bumped my head. I thought I'd wake up from the dream of being in this strange place and time, but that never happened. I just wandered through the tunnels and the waterfront for what seemed like weeks. It was actually only twenty-eight hours.

"I was hungry and dirty when Delores found me and took me home with her. Her parents were as kind as she was.

"Mr. Faraday, Delores's father, asked at the different businesses on the waterfront about my parents. I couldn't tell him it was no use. What was I supposed to say? That they weren't even born yet? Delores and I spent day after day searching for the bricks, but after months passed, I gave up hope." Tears rolled down Bertha's cheeks and her eyes were shiny.

The carriage driver turned in his seat. "It's a bit early in the day for ghost stories, isn't it?" He grinned.

Sam clenched her fists. What a jerk. She leaned forward. "Lis—"

"Mind your business, sir, and we will do the same." Grandma's sharp retort wiped the grin off the man's face. He tipped his hat and clucked to the horses. She nodded to Bertha. "Go on, Dear."

"Delores started introducing me as her cousin visiting from New Jersey, and I resigned myself to my new life." Bertha sighed. "Delores and I never found the bricks. Not until you girls arrived, that is."

Nicole reached out to Bertha. "You can go home now, with us."

"You are too kind." Bertha took Nicole's hand and kissed it. "I missed my mother so much. I still do, and I guess I could go home, but it wouldn't be home anymore. I'm an old woman. I've spent most of my life here, and this is all I know." Bertha smiled at Grandma tears glistening on her cheeks.

Sam wiped her forehead with her sleeve. Was the

evening getting hotter instead of cooling off? If they didn't hurry, Bertha's reality would become her own. Nicole's too. Sam shook her head. "But if you used the bricks—"

"What is your mother and father's name?" Nicole asked.

"Donald and Elise Welby."

"Welby? Aunt Eli?" She gripped her stomach.

"Bertha, my dear." Grandma patted Bertha's arm.

Elise wrung her hands, "Driver, hurry."

Chapter 20

Race Against Time

The horses stopped in front of a brick building with Seamstresses over one of the plate glass windows. Two women were coming out. Grandma put some coins in the driver's hand and stepped to the ground. She rushed to the seamstress shop and entered.

She waved to the clerk. "Hi, Mabel. Just need to go down for a couple minutes. Do you mind?"

Mabel's eyes widened as Sam, Henri, Nicole, Bertha, and Elise tromped through her store and to a door in the back corner. "I'll be here until after midnight tonight finishing Miss Ladd's wedding dress alterations, so take your time."

"We will be finished well before then." Grandma held the door open.

Elise led everyone down into the tunnels. Mr. Stickel sat leaning against the wall with Sally standing over him with her stick.

"It's about time you got here, Elise." Stickel moved to stand, and Sally waved her stick at him. "Drat you, woman."

Music from a piano filtered through the floor, and Elise ignored Stickel and motioned for Henri. "Do you have your key?"

"Here." Henri unlocked the door, and they all filed

into the Lucky Star stockroom. Sam scrunched against the wall that held the bricks. She glared at Elise. Grandma pushed past her into the room followed by Bertha. Sally let Mr. Stickel rise to his feet and entered the room. He walked to a corner.

Woman after woman shuffled in the crowded stockroom, and dust rose to fill the air. Sam coughed. The glow of the bricks changed from green to gold but were still pale. Why did Elise hesitate? Couldn't she do this one thing?

"All Nicole and I want to do is to go home, and the bricks are right there." Sam pointed to the bricks and the glow became brighter. "Please."

"I know, dear, but without Freddie, I'm afraid there's nothing we can do." Grandma gazed at Sam, and Sam could feel the warmth rising from her neck to her cheeks. Of course, they needed Freddie, but she wanted to go home. What was it about the bricks?

"I see it now…how Bertha got left behind." Grandma placed a hand on Elise's arm. "It was when your father disappeared. The bricks were activated, allowing Bertha to use them. And she ended up here, just like Sam and Nicole."

"Wait." Sam put a hand to her head. "Did I miss something? How could Bertha use the bricks?" A pain developed behind her eyes, and she clenched her teeth. The bricks would drive her crazy too, just like Stickel.

Grandma lowered her voice. "Who is your mother, Bertha?"

Bertha set the book on a crate of rum, lavender perfuming the air. "Eleanor Weber, you kno—"

"Aunt Eli?" Sam's knees buckled. "You are Aunt Eli's—"

"Daughter. We had no way of knowing for sure, but now it is clear. We are related." Bertha stared at Grandma. "We were related all along?"

"We could not know for sure. It took someone from the future to fill in that piece of the puzzle. It all makes sense now." Grandma's hands shook as she reached for her friend.

Sam shook her head. How could Aunt Eli be Bertha's mother? "I thought her daughter died. How could this have happened?"

"I am not certain, and we may never know." Grandma frowned. "You said the bricks were shimmering, right Bertha?"

"We've gone over the details a thousand times. Yes, the bricks glowed. I touched them. I landed in this very room in 1861."

"What was going through your mind when you touched the bricks?" Elise asked. "I think that may be more important than anything else." All eyes were on Bertha.

"Hmph, no one asked me that question, and to tell you the truth, I wish I could forget the answer because I've regretted my petty thoughts on that day, every day since." Bertha dabbed her eyes with her hanky. "I was angry and wanted my parents to understand how they had ruined my life. We had moved to a new neighborhood. I was only thirteen, remember. I didn't have any friends, and all I wanted was acceptance, a sense of belonging, just one person my age to talk to."

"I was your age." Grandma held Bertha's hand. "Why didn't you tell me this before? Intention is as important as anything when it comes to the bricks. We know that now."

Bertha wiped her eyes with her kerchief. "I didn't want anyone to know how selfish I'd been, and I knew it was my own fault. I'd done this to myself, and even though I was only alone for two days when you found me, I was terrified."

Sam cringed. She'd only wanted to get Dad back, but she'd been selfish, and Nicole had suffered ever since.

"We cannot change the past, Bertha." Grandma put a hand on Bertha's shoulder.

"Not for me, but we can make sure this doesn't happen again." Bertha glanced at Nicole and Sam. "You want to go home, right?" Her eyes softened as she spoke.

"We do want to go home." Nicole squeezed Sam's hand.

"Something is different this time, though." Grandma tapped her chin with a finger. "From the beginning, this was an imperfect spell. I think it was tainted by Charles's inability to love, and that is why he must be present." She gazed at Bertha and then Elise. "I know you both blame yourselves for what happened, but you cannot, and I know you do not want Charles here, but he must be." She glared at Stickel.

"It's not my fault Freddie trusted me." Stickel returned Grandma's glare.

"It most certainly is, and if that boy is missing one hair on his head—" Grandma shook a fist at him. "You have tampered with time, Charles, and your inability to love is what caused this mess."

Bertha nodded. "Hopefully, with Freddie's and Elise's help, we can cleanse the channels, and correct the pathway for your safe return."

The scent of lavender grew stronger and stronger in

the enclosed space. Sam put a hand to her head to stop it from spinning. "So, when Bertha touched the bricks, she traveled back in time but to a time before the spell had been cast, but I did the same thing, only I brought my best friend with me." Her stomach rolled and she bent over. "Touching the bricks was the worst decision of my life." She glanced from Henri to Elise, Grandma, Nicole, and Mr. Stickel surrounded by his female guards.

Elise clasped her hands to her chest. "What is taking Red and Freddie so long?"

****

The Lucky Star stockroom walls pressed in on Sam as she paced back and forth. It must be almost midnight. If Freddie didn't arrive soon, she and Nicole would grow old here just like Bertha. She could see the resemblance to Aunt Eli now, the high forehead, the arching eyebrows. Poor Aunt Eli, no wonder she seldom smiled. Was that why Bertha never smiled? They were related, all of them.

The bricks were growing dimmer.

Glancing at Nicole, Sam tried to envision her as an old woman like Bertha. Bertha had missed out on birthdays, Christmases, and family. Would Nicole miss those things too? Sam slumped against the wall. She'd touched those bricks without a thought for what might happen to Nicole. She'd wanted Dad back, but she'd solved nothing. Dad was still gone, and her only hope of getting home rested in the wisdom of her ancestors, Grandma, Elise, Freddie, and Bertha.

If they couldn't help her, no one could, and if Freddie didn't hurry, it wouldn't matter. She sighed. If only she could tell Aunt Eli, she'd found Bertha.

"Footsteps," Bertha whispered.

The door burst open and Red, Archie, and another man who looked more like her father than Big Jim even. Freddie? Maybe she would get home after all.

"Freddie." Elise's eyes rolled back in her head, as she slumped to the floor.

Chapter 21

No Place Like Home

Bertha sank beside Elise on the floor. She lifted Elise's head into her lap. "Tsk. You baby these kids." She shook her head at Grandma. With Bertha's help, Elise sat up, and Red took hold of her arm and helped her to stand. Bertha rose to hold Elise's other arm.

Grandma ignored Bertha. "Oh, Freddie, you're just in time. We must send these girls back to their own time and deactivate the bricks once and for all"

"Freddie, my boy, I am glad to see you well." Mr. Stickel's eyes were bright, and his voice echoed off the walls. He giggled and began to whistle.

Sally held up her broom handle ready to strike. Sam didn't move.

Freddie walked to the wall and gazed at the bricks as their glow diminished. "We have no time to lose. Elise?" Freddie reached a hand to her.

"Where's Big Jim?" Red scanned the room, his eyes darting over every keg and box.

"I thought he was with you." Grandma brushed the dust from her skirt and Sam saw that she was avoiding eye contact. "I haven't seen him since he raced after Mr. Stickel."

Did Grandma know more than she was telling? Sam didn't care. She just wanted to go home. If this worked, she'd have to get Dad to come home another way, but right now, she'd just have to trust in the bricks and her family.

"I see he got Stickel, and that is what matters. I can take it from here, ladies." Red stood guard as Stickel frowned up at him.

Why didn't Red handcuff him? Henri moved to her father, and he placed his arm around her. All Henri wanted from the beginning was her father, and now she had him. She'd kept her promise to Henri, and now she had to keep her promise to Nicole.

"Okay, people." Grandma clapped her hands. Bertha stood at her right-hand side as though they'd done this before, but how could that be? "We only have until midnight, and it is, oh my—"

"It is 11:50." Bertha clicked her pocket watch shut and slipped it into her pocket.

"Elise, you stand here, Freddie here, Sam here." Grandma moved each of them until they formed a triangle. "And Nicole, you place your hand on Sam's shoulder."

Bertha held up the book and read. "Now, everyone stand back, and do not touch them."

Sam looked at Elise and Freddie. The air seemed to vibrate, and the bricks pulsed and began to glow brighter.

"Back, you scoundrel." Archie held Stickel's arm as he reached for Sam.

"You are fired, by the way." Stickel glared at Archie.

Grandma pointed at Stickel. "You will not interfere this time."

Sam shook her pounding head. This had been the longest day of her life, and all she wanted was to go home. Now that would be a great birthday gift—

But her birthday wasn't until tomorrow. Was she going to get her birthday back? Maybe there'd be waffles.

"Elise, you and Frederick must speak the spell one last time. This will send the girls to the future then the bricks will become dormant."

Stickel stood, pulling against Archie's grip. Could he hold Stickel?

"Sam, be ready to touch the bricks when I say. Nicole, do not lose contact with Sam."

"This is an attempt?" Nicole's voice trembled. "I plan on succeeding here."

"We will succeed." Sam nodded, gazing into Nicole's brown eyes. "We will be home in less than a minute, right Grandma?"

"That's right, dear." Grandma nodded.

Nicole's chin started to quiver and soon she was blubbering like a baby.

"Now what?" Sam asked.

"I don't know. I'm going miss Henri, Paul, Will, Misa, and especially Bertha. Oh, and Grandma and Elise, and even Big Jim and the way Red sighs every time Elise walks in the room." Tears ran down Nicole's face.

Elise cleared her throat, her face turning crimson. Red grinned.

"Wait. I see something." Sam pushed past Grandma.

"I thought you wanted to go home?" Grandma reached to grab Sam's arm, but Sam pulled away.

"Misa?" Sam saw others with her.

"Yes. It is I." Misa bowed. "Paul and Will came too with some of the girls you helped save from the *Palisade Pearl*."

"We wanted to thank you for saving our friends." Paul pulled his hat off his head. Will grinned over his shoulder.

Sam and Nicole grinned at one another, and tears streamed down Nicole's face. Sam wiped her nose on her sleeve. "Don't start, Nicole, because I won't be able to stop."

Grandma cleared her throat. "Do you want to go home or not?"

Sam nodded. "Yes. I do, but—"

"Then say your goodbyes and dry your eyes because time flies."

A rhyme? She'd miss Grandma with all her quirks. She bowed to Misa and waved to Paul and Will. Then she nodded to Grandma and positioned herself next to Elise and Frederick.

Bertha cleared her throat. "Recite the lines and let us end this chapter of the bricks."

Elise and Frederick held hands and reached for the bricks. Nicole held onto Sam's shoulder.

Elise began to recite the lines, as the bricks hummed. They seemed almost liquid.

> *Ancestors we bow on bended knee*
> *And ask you with our loving plea*
> *Our hands upon these bricks of clay*
> *Transport us through the misty array*

Freddie followed:
> *Awaken portals of ancient rite*
> *With our touch as we alight*

They both recited the last two lines:

Our hands upon these bricks of clay
Transport us through the misty array
Freddie whispered, "Seattle."

Sam imagined Seattle and the underground tunnel where this had all begun. She imagined her mother and father together, and the key and the lavender note destroyed. She glanced at Nicole as Stickel reached one last time and Archie pulled him back.

Grandma held her clasped hands up as if in prayer. "*Now.*"

Nicole's hand gripped her shoulder as she reached toward the bricks.

"God speed, dears." Grandma winked at her.

"Goodbye." She blinked back tears and pressed her hand over Freddie's and Elise's.

A familiar whoosh of air pulled from her lungs and a small tug pulled her off balance.

Chapter 22

The Present

Dust rose and the room swirled. Sam wiped her eyes. The same bare light bulb illuminated the room. Electricity. They were home.

"We're back?" Nicole sat on the floor.

"But is this the right time, and where are the bricks?" She scanned the walls and paused. They still glowed but grew dimmer and dimmer until they faded to the same dull color as the other bricks. "It worked. The bricks are gone."

"Well, Bertha did say their magic would end at midnight." Nicole pulled out her phone. "I have bars. This is our time."

"Wait. Who are you calling?" Should she stop her? What were they going to say? They better work out a story.

"I was going to call Mom, but I'm not sure what to tell her? 'Hi, Mom. Just got back from 1901.' " Nicole sighed. "I just want to sleep in my own bed." Nicole jumped fumbling her phone as it started pinging loading all the messages that couldn't reach her in 1901.

"Hey, Sam." Nicole stared at the wall where the bricks no longer glowed. "Didn't Henri say it was July 6, 1901, when we landed in Portland?"

"It was." Sam's head swam with understanding.

"Wait. Do you mean...?

"We were too busy trying to survive to consider what that meant. But now it makes sense, right?"

Sam stared at the wall—no glow, no pulse. "The magic of the bricks ran out at midnight so we wouldn't run into ourselves in 1901. We haven't even left yet."

"You're right. That's kind of genius, really. Do you think that was part of the spell?" Nicole put a hand to her mouth and glanced at her phone. She stared at Sam.

"What?" Sam wasn't sure she wanted to hear whatever it was Nicole would say next. Couldn't the bricks leave her alone?

"It's midnight on the night before the field trip." Light glistened in Nicole's eyes, wide as saucers. "Sam, we get a do-over."

Sam stepped back, pulling Nicole into the shadows. "Someone's coming."

Footsteps pounded down the tunnel, and Sam gripped Nicole's hand as they crouched in the shadows behind a beam. A figure rushed into the room, tall and familiar. "Sam?"

"Dad?"

****

Sam stared out the bus window at the tall brick buildings of Pioneer Square. The sky was a deep blue just like the last time she'd experienced July 7th. She sighed. Do-overs were the best, especially when it was a birthday because the first time doing this one sucked. Sam grinned. The last time she'd been here she had wanted to be anywhere else, but today this was the only place she wanted to be, heading to the Old Pioneers Underground Tour, where she would touch nothing.

Dad had made her chocolate chip birthday waffles,

and Mom smiled as though the key had never existed. Sam hugged her before running out to catch the bus, her perma-smile cramping her cheeks, but that was a small price to pay for a perfect birthday breakfast. It was like magic. The fight had never happened. She had won the birthday-lottery, for sure.

She inhaled the fresh Seattle air. What could go wrong? The bricks were dormant, and she wasn't touching anything today.

A warm breeze brushed her face as she stepped off the bus. She walked with Nicole across Pioneer Park to Doc Maynard's Public House. She shivered. This was the strangest déjà vu she'd ever had. She glanced at the ally and blinked. Who was that standing at the corner of the building?

"Nicole look." Sam pointed to a rotund, old man in a torn and soiled suit. The blood in her veins pounded, and Nicole gasped as they stared at the figure twisting his hat. He was mumbling something. Sam shivered. "Did he just say, 'Nome?' "

"It's probably just something homeless guys say, right?" Nicole's voice squeaked.

"But it looks like Sti…?"

Nicole put a hand on Sam's shoulder and shook her head. Sam turned back to stare at the grizzled face of the man.

"Today we get a re-do," Nicole hissed. "Remember?"

"Sam. Nicole. This way please." Mrs. Phelps broke the spell.

Nicole giggled, and Sam bit her bottom lip and nodded. This was do-over day, right? Phelps motioned them to follow their classmates inside Doc Maynard's.

There would be no *déjà vu* today.

Sam took one more glance at the corner, but the man was gone. She sighed and followed Nicole. This would be a boring, *normal* day. It had to be.

****

The streetlights illuminated a quiet, tree-lined street with houses behind hedges and shrubs. James glanced up and down the sidewalks, and detecting no movement, he stepped out of his car and reached into the back seat. He lifted the package. He'd wrapped it in plain brown paper and didn't take it home this time. He was an old dog who could learn from his mistakes. He glanced at the night sky, the full moon shining over Seattle. He knocked on the door at house number 377, admiring, as he always did, the white-framed windows, a stark contrast to the solid brick walls that rose into the dark night.

"Just like a castle," Sam always said.

Aunt Eli called, "It's unlocked. Come in."

He opened the door and strode into the foyer carrying the package. The last time he'd entered this house, he'd left clutching a key with a lavender-scented cord, which sent Carol into a frenzy of tears. This time, he'd left his wife sleeping peacefully. Then he'd said good night to Sam. Jim grinned. She was home and safe, but how would he ever answer all of her questions?

He hung his coat on a coat rack and strode into the living room, the package under his arm. He bent to kiss the woman sitting dwarfed by her overstuffed chair, purple afghan across her lap, the scent of lavender filling the air. Her orange tabby rose, jumped from her lap, stretched, and blinked his amber eyes at Jim. The fireplace crackled casting a yellow hue on the walls and ceiling.

"How are the names?" He patted the cat. The Duke had done his part to perfection.

"The names are back. Congratulations, James. I knew you could do it."

"Good, because I had my doubts."

"I never had a one." She beamed at him.

"It wasn't until Sam arrived that everything came together. That's when Red and Elise met."

"It was the key. You didn't even realize you'd dropped it.

"No. I was too upset. Carol…"

"I know that was hard for you." Aunt Eli motioned for Jim to sit.

"I have to get home.

She smiled and nodded. "Stickel really altered the spell, didn't he?"

Jim's throat tightened. "If Sam hadn't followed with the key, I wouldn't be standing here now."

"But she did follow you, and she's home now, sleeping in her own bed. Hard to believe all that happened in under twenty-four hours."

"It probably seemed much longer to her. She was exhausted when we got home." Jim chuckled.

Aunt Eli sighed and blinked at Jim. "How was Delores and—"

"Delores is, well—Delores, but Bertha stayed behind. You knew she would."

Aunt Eli clasped her hands. "My poor girl. I miss her so, but yes. I knew she would stay. Too much time had passed." She dabbed the tears from her eyes.

"At least she knows now that she's been surrounded by family this whole time. That's some consolation." James patted the package in his hand before placing it in her lap. "Now, will you destroy this package this time? We can't have another disappearing-names-episode."

"Of course, James. I'll take care of it." Aunt Eli closed her eyes as James leaned down to kiss her brow.

He nodded and turned to leave. He glanced over his shoulder. She sat in the chair so tiny and frail, but she was sly. He shrugged into his coat and opened the door. She would destroy them this time.

****

Aunt Eli gripped the package with one hand and the banister with the other. She used to run up and down these stairs but look at her now. She leaned her cane at the top and made her way, one step at a time. The Duke brushed against her leg.

"Yes. Yes. I'm coming." She shuffled across the basement floor and pulled a painting of the Columbia Gorge back to reveal a safe as the Duke weaved between her legs. She smiled. Jim could offer suggestions, but the bricks were her responsibility, not his, not yet. Spinning the dial, she counted out the numbers, left, right, then left. She turned the handle and the door clicked open.

"The disappearing names could have destroyed us all, eh?" Aunt Eli glanced at the cat, then placed the package in the safe.

The Duke sat licking his paws as she shut the door, turned the dial to scramble the code, and recovered the safe with the painting. "I never had any doubts in James's ability, but he could never have solved this problem without that key. Sam's entrance saved the day. What a pleasant surprise. James and Sam will make a good team, don't you think?" Aunt Eli smiled down at the orange tabby. "My time is almost come to an end, my friend. But you'll enjoy living here with James and Sam once I'm gone, won't you?"

"The bricks must never be destroyed, and Jim will understand that soon enough."

The Duke blinked his amber eyes once and yawned.

"Guillem would be so proud of you, my friend. You've saved this family once again." She sighed. "What would we ever do without you? Thank you."

"Meow." The Duke stretched arching his back before curling into a ball on his bed below the safe.

Aunt Eli bent down, stroked the Duke's sleek orange fur, then stood and placed her palm on the painting covering the safe.

She ambled across the room, and placing her foot on the first step, she glanced back. Sir Archibald, the Duke of Pisica lay with his head upon his paws, but he gazed at her with his amber eyes and winked. She nodded, grinning as she climbed the stairs.

A word about the author...

Avis M. Adams lives in the Pacific Northwest and writes poetry, young adult and middle-grade novels. She dabbles in picture books and produces poetry that incorporates the beauty of the region. She is an award-winning poet and Quilcene, her first book of poetry was released in 2019. She is a member of PNWA and was a finalist in the YA and Picture Book categories of their literary contest. She teaches English courses at Green River College, presents at conferences, gardens, and enjoys travel and the great outdoors. The Incident, her debut YA novel released in 2022 from The Wild Rose Press.

She also writes romance, and her first romance novella, The Christmas Wish Knotts will be released before Christmas 2022! https://avis-m-adams.com

Thank you for purchasing
this publication of The Wild Rose Press, Inc.

For questions or more information
contact us at
info@thewildrosepress.com.

The Wild Rose Press, Inc.
www.thewildrosepress.com

Lightning Source UK Ltd.
Milton Keynes UK
UKHW020651210223
417383UK00014B/447